AN ALO NUDGER MYSTERY

THE RIGHT TO SING THE BLUES

Two-time Shamus Award-winner JOHN LUTZ has produced more than thirty novels and 200 short stories, becoming "one of the most reliable pros of American P.I. writing," according to *The Washington Post*. His *SWFSeeks Same* was the basis for the 1992 movie *Single White Female* starring Bridget Fonda. A former president of both the Mystery Writers of America and the Private Eye Writers of America, he was awarded Lifetime Achievement honors from the PWA in 1995. Lutz lives in Webster Groves, Missouri, where he once worked as a switchboard operator for the St. Louis Metropolitan Police Department.

AVAILABLE NOW

Alfred Hitchcock Mysteries
The Vertigo Murders
by J. Madison Davis

Alo Nudger Mysteries
by John Lutz
Nightlines

Amos Walker Mysteries
by Loren D. Estleman
Motor City Blue
Angel Eyes
The Midnight Man
The Glass Highway

Moses Wine Mysteries
by Roger L. Simon
The Big Fix
Wild Turkey
Peking Duck
The Lost Coast

Masao Masuto Mysteries
by Howard Fast
Masuto Investigates

Otto Penzler Hollywood Mysteries
Laura
by Vera Caspary

Philip Marlowe Mysteries
Raymond Chandler's Philip Marlowe
Anthology; Byron Preiss, Editor

Sherlock Holmes Mysteries
Revenge of the Hound
by Michael Hardwick

Sherlock Holmes vs. Dracula
by Loren D. Estleman

Toby Peters Mysteries
by Stuart M. Kaminsky
Murder on the Yellow Brick Road
The Devil Met a Lady
Never Cross a Vampire

COMING SOON

Sugartown
An Amos Walker Mystery
by Loren D. Estleman

She Done Him Wrong
A Toby Peters Mystery
by Stuart M. Kaminsky

THE RIGHT TO SING THE BLUES

JOHN LUTZ

ibooks
new york
www.ibooksinc.com

DISTRIBUTED BY SIMON & SCHUSTER, INC

THE RIGHT TO
SING THE BLUES

There's Music in all things, if men had ears:
Their earth is but an echo of the spheres.
—Lord Byron
Don Juan

Why should the devil have all the good tunes?
—Rowland Hill
Sermons

I

Nudger belched and said, " 'S'cuse me."

"You want some more coffee, Nudge?"

Danny asked, pausing as he wiped down the stainless-steel counter with the grayish towel he usually kept tucked in his belt. He looked over at Nudger with his somber basset-hound eyes, concerned eyes. "Maybe it'd help to settle your stomach."

Maybe it would eat a hole through my entire digestive tract, Nudger thought. But he said, "No, thanks, Danny," and thumbed back the foil on a roll of antacid tablets. He popped one of the chalky white disks into his mouth and gazed down at what was left of his Danny's Dunker Delite before him on the counter.

He was eating breakfast at Danny's Donuts because Danny would let him postpone payment indefinitely. For this Nudger was grateful. But he had braved a Dunker Delite four mornings in a row now, and he was afraid that if this culinary daring continued, he'd begin to look like one of the formidable specials served at Danny's Donuts; he might become as round and polysaturated as a Dunker Delite, and not nearly so hard.

He lifted his foam cup to take a sip of Danny's horrendous coffee and wished the private-investigation business would pick up. Didn't sultry blondes in distress wander into PIs' offices anymore? Then talk a while, pout a while, flirt a while, and pay a generous retainer?

Of course, he might never find out unless he went upstairs to his office. Not much business of any kind was transpiring here at Danny's counter.

Nudger didn't feel like trudging upstairs to his bare desk, inanity-loaded answering machine, dusty file cabinets, and silent phone. It all reminded him of the overdue rent.

Danny knew why Nudger was breakfasting at the doughnut shop. "Things'll get better, Nudge," he said, expertly snapping the towel to flick a stubborn crumb off the counter. There was no one else in the place, and hadn't been since the last secretary from the building across the street had left with her grease-spotted box of a dozen glazed to-go. How Danny stayed in business was more of a mystery than Nudger could solve. "You know how it goes," Danny added. "Just when you think you're at the end of your rope, somehow you find a way to pull yourself up."

"Unless there's a noose at the end of the rope," Nudger said.

Danny ignored him and drew himself a large cup of coffee from the big steel urn. He had a frequent-user's immunity to the stuff. "Like last year, when our esteemed landlord was about to evict me," he said, leaning on the counter and testing the steaming coffee with his fingertip. "I really thought I was gonna have to toss in the towel, then along came the cream horns."

Nudger looked up from his coffee. "Cream horns?"

"Yeah, a thousand of 'em. This little gal who worked at the K-Mart up the street used to come down here every day and buy one of my cream horns for her lunch. She loved the things. Then I didn't see her for a while, and I heard she got engaged to some rich lawyer out in Ladue. Well, she wanted my cream horns served at her wedding reception. She came in here the week before the wedding and placed an order for a thousand cream horns. Saved my business."

"Something old, something blue," Nudger said.

"Huh?"

"Nothing, Danny." Nudger swiveled and stood up from his stool. His lower back ached from sitting too long slumped over. "I'll be upstairs waiting to hear from someone who needs a thousand cream horns traced."

"You never know, Nudge."

"It seems that way sometimes. See you later, Danny."

Carrying his half-cup of coffee, Nudger pushed out the door into the morning heat. He made a sharp U-turn and went through another door, right next to Danny's, that opened onto the narrow, steep stairway up to his office.

As he climbed the creaking stairs, he splashed coffee onto his thumb and cursed. He stooped to pick up the mail on the landing, unlocked his office door, went inside, and switched on the window air conditioner before he did anything else. It was nine-thirty in the morning and the office was hot enough to bake a potato; a typical July day in St. Louis, home of the Heat Alert.

He tossed the mail on the desk and sat down in his squealing swivel chair, braced for its shrill *Good-Morneeeng*. He shoved the foam coffee cup away in distaste. The cool draft from the humming, gurgling air conditioner danced between the spokes of his chair, over his damp shoulder blades.

While he waited to get cool, he regarded the pile of mail. Finally he picked it up from the desk and leafed through it.

There were no surprises, only offers to buy accident insurance, subscribe to magazines, tour lakeside property, enter the *Reader's Digest* $100,000 sweepstakes. Damn!—the electric bill. Nudger studied it and wondered how much electricity a secondhand IBM typewriter and a used window air conditioner actually consumed.

Whoops!

A white envelope Nudger hadn't noticed slipped out from between the insurance pitch and the offer of a free camera for touring Paradise Estates, flipped once in midair, and bounced off the toe of his shoe. Even through the shoe he could tell that it was heavy, and he could see that the address was handwritten and not typed or printed on a label. Maybe it was worth opening.

Nudger leaned forward in the squealing swivel chair and scooped up the envelope. It was plastered with stamps and had a New Orleans postmark. There was no return address. Nudger's office address was written in a bold yet flowery hand, dashed off with a thick felt-tipped blue pen. He hefted the envelope, leaned back, and tore open the sealed flap.

The envelope contained a round-trip airline ticket to New Orleans, first class, in Nudger's name. The flight left St. Louis at 11:05 the next morning.

Nudger dug in the envelope and came up with a folded note and a business card. The note was brief and written on plain white paper in the same flowery handwriting used on the envelope.

Nudger, my man,

I need the services of a private investigator. Let's talk in person as soon as you get into New Orleans. The Hotel Majestueux is holding a room in your name. Phone me when you arrive and we'll meet. This will be worth your while. If you hear me out and then disagree, fly again home. You have nothing to lose. I have everything to lose. Come talk to a worried man with money. Please.

Fat Jack McGee

The card was engraved with a logo of a clarinet emitting a cartoon swirl of musical notes. It was also engraved with "Fat Jack McGee," a New Orleans address, and two phone numbers.

Fat Jack McGee. The clarinet.

Nudger knew about Fat Jack McGee, had several of his records cut in the sixties and early seventies in his jazz collection. Like many gifted jazz musicians, though not known to the general public, Fat Jack was one of the elite in the jazz world. He had played clarinet with his own band for years, then semi-retired to a jazz club he'd bought in New Orleans. While he still composed music for other musicians, some of them pop stars, he no longer recorded, and from what Nudger had read he performed for his paying customers only occasionally. All in all, his was an accomplished and lucrative career.

Nudger knew how Fat Jack had acquired money. He wondered how he'd acquired worry.

He also wondered if it was worth going to New Orleans to find out. Benedict and Schill, a couple of lawyers Nudger sometimes worked for, had promised to throw him some business at the end of their next ambulance chase. If Nudger left the city, he might miss that opportunity and waste several days in New Orleans while his rent rolled on. The Fat Jack McGee thing might already be solved or have evaporated by the time Nudger showed up. Or McGee could simply change his mind about hiring a private investigator. Benedict and Schill had come through before. Fat Jack McGee hadn't, except on long-playing albums.

The phone jangled, making Nudger jump and the swivel chair cry *Eek*!

He waited three rings before answering; mustn't seem anxious. Then he dragged the phone across the desk toward him, lifted the receiver, and with a heart full of hope identified himself.

"It's me," said his former wife Eileen. "You know why I'm calling."

Nudger knew. "Not our anniversary?"

"I don't want to make tiny, tiny small talk," she said. "I want the back alimony you owe me. Five hundred dollars."

"Right now, that isn't possible," Nudger said.

"Hauling you back into court *is* possible."

Nudger wasn't really sure she would do that. The alimony she'd been granted was exorbitant, thanks to her lawyer who had descended from sharks. And though Eileen didn't have the means to earn a living at the time of the divorce, she was now at the top of a sales pyramid in one of those home products rackets, drawing an obscene percentage of the earnings of the salespeople under her, plus a commission whenever they recruited someone into the company. She was a district manager. Pyramid Power was hers. She was making a better living than Nudger was now, or ever had, for that matter. Surely a judge would take that into consideration. Well, maybe . . .

"Are you there?"

"Here."

"I talked with my lawyer. He says give you a week, then we'll skin you alive and scrape the fat off your hide."

"He has a way of putting things."

"And of getting things. I don't want to spend more time in court, but I will if I have to. I want my money. Soon." She'd sure gotten assertive since getting into sales. She seemed especially voracious today.

"Will you send cash? Or a check?"

Nudger sighed. "A check. As soon as possible."

"Which will be?"

"Days. Weeks at the most. I'm getting a retainer soon."

"Probably to straighten your teeth with my money."

"No, the other kind of retainer. I've got a job in New Orleans. And my teeth are straight."

"Okay, you've got one week," she said. "And no more. Seven days. Understand?"

"Sure. Are you getting any sex, Eileen?" He just had to aggravate her, couldn't stop himself. Sick.

As she slammed down the receiver she shouted something he couldn't understand, but it had the word "God" in it. Could she have found religion?

Nudger listened to the lonely sound of the broken connection for a few seconds, then replaced the receiver. Nothing like having your mind made up for you. He phoned the airport to confirm his reservation for New Orleans, and a very pleasant woman named Rhonda assured him that he was booked first class. Nudger locked the airline ticket in his top desk drawer, thinking he'd rather talk on the phone to Rhonda than Eileen any day.

He diligently filled out the $100,000 sweepstakes form, then, whistling out of tune, went downstairs to get another cup of coffee and a cream horn.

II

The flight to New Orleans took a little over an hour in a sky as uniformly blue and unmarred as the inside of a fine china bowl.

Nudger rented a car—a cheap subcompact, since he didn't know if he'd take this job and have his expenses covered—at New Orleans International Airport and drove toward the city. Louisiana was just as hot as Missouri, only here Spanish moss drooped from the roadside trees like gloomy black Christmas tinsel somebody had forgotten to take down. Just looking at the graceful yet oppressive stuff made the heat seem fiercer and stickier. Nudger reached out and switched the little red car's air conditioner on high. Dust and debris blew up into his face with the sudden blast of cold air, then settled back down rearranged.

New Orleans is an old city of pastel stucco, ornate black wrought iron, colorful clinging bougainvillea, white-and-gray tropical-weight clothing, French-Cajun cooking, and black music. The Hotel Majestueux fit right into that scene, an old ten-story building with a fake but weathered stucco facade. There was a gold awning out over the sidewalk in front of the entrance, with the name of the hotel lettered in delicate white script along the sides. A uniformed doorman stood in the deep shade beneath the awning, studiously reading a folded newspaper.

Nudger parked the subcompact half a block down, climbed from the tiny bucket seat, and checked to make sure his limbs would still extend to their fullest. Subcompactness could be catching. He unlocked the car's miniature trunk and got out his luggage.

As he carried his single brown nylon suitcase toward the hotel, he looked over the neighborhood. It was old, gone a measure to seed, but not all that bad. The Chamber of Commerce would describe it as colorful. Tourists would agree, but would spend their money on Bourbon Street and at the Superdome.

"Carry that for you, sir?" the doorman asked, when it became apparent that Nudger was about to enter the lobby with his suitcase.

Nudger declined by shaking his head no and walked on past. Up close, the doorman's ornate uniform had the same genteel seediness about it as the neighborhood. He was an elderly black man, wiry and stooped. It was a racing form he'd been studying, Nudger noted, as he pushed open the glass doors. The doorman didn't look as if he had an eye for winners.

The Majestueux lobby was large, carpeted in red, and furnished in a kind of hotel French provincial that lent an air of hominess. There was plenty of aged oak paneling, setting off large potted ferns and flowering plants that looked real. A fancy brass clock and elaborate brass floor indicators were built into rich paneling above the elevator doors. Behind the polished wood desk loomed a seven-foot-tall, narrow, gray-haired man. A bellman was on the far side of the lobby doing something to a stuck window to make it go either farther up or farther down. With a kind of condescending nobility, a tall Creole beauty dressed in the manner of a restaurant hostess stood with her arms crossed in the doorway of the hotel coffee shop and idly watched the bellman's efforts. Another bellman was behind her, looking out over her shoulder. Nobody here rushed to take Nudger's luggage.

The human tower behind the desk checked and said sure enough, there was a reservation in Nudger's name. Nudger produced his VISA card, wondering if he had enough credit left on it to impress the desk clerk if it became necessary.

But there was no need for clout here. The clerk shook his cadaverous narrow head and said, "Room's been prepaid, Mr. Nudger."

While Nudger returned the credit card to his wallet, the tall guy slapped a big old-fashioned desk bell. It had too beautiful and resonating a ring to serve such a mundane purpose. The clerk yelled, "Front," in a brisk, commanding voice, and the bellman by the window tore himself away from his handyman puttering and started to walk across the lobby toward the desk.

"Three-oh-four, Larry," the desk clerk said from on high.

Larry took the key from him and picked up Nudger's suitcase. He was a chunky, medium-height man with thick raven-black hair and a mottled complexion like heavily creamed coffee that hadn't been stirred. Pausing to avoid a young couple with the self-involved look of honeymooners, he stepped nimbly around them into the elevator, punched a floor button, and moved back to make room for Nudger.

The third-floor room was large, on the verge of needing redecorating, but on the whole very pleasant. It was done in shades of blue, with thick draperies that matched the bedspread. The headboard, dresser, and writing desk didn't match and were of heavy walnut construction, not the usual mass-produced hotel furnishings. Larry smoothly showed Nudger that the color TV worked, introduced him to the white-tiled bathroom but not the small roach that scurried behind the washbasin, then handed over the room key.

Larry had black, intense eyes. He hadn't said a word, and maybe he couldn't talk, but he was a hell of a watcher. Nudger tipped him two dollars, eager to be rid of his presence. Larry grunted as he pocketed the bills, shot a mechanical smile in Nudger's direction, and backed out of the room, closing the door behind him. Nudger walked over and slid the bolt home, locking the door from the inside.

He unpacked hurriedly, then turned down the thermostat on the window air conditioner and removed his sport coat. From an inside pocket of the coat he drew the envelope Fat Jack McGee had sent him, then draped the coat on the back of the desk chair. With the envelope's contents spread before him on the bed, he reread the letter. Then he picked up the Touch-Tone phone from the bedside table and with his forefinger pecked out the office number printed on Fat Jack McGee's thick white business card. It was time to arrange that meeting the rotund jazz legend wanted so badly.

"There's this that you need to know about jazz," Fat Jack told Nudger an hour later. "You don't need to know a thing about it to enjoy it, and that's all you need to know." He tossed back his huge head, jowls quivering, and drained the final sip of brandy from his crystal snifter. "It's feel," he said across the table to Nudger, using a white napkin to dab at his lips with a very fat man's peculiar delicacy. "Jazz is pure feel."

"Does Willy Hollister have the feel?" Nudger asked. He pushed his plate away, feeling full to the point of being bloated. The only portion of the gourmet lunch Fat Jack had bought him that remained untouched was the grits, which Nudger didn't think belonged on the plate to begin with. Fat Jack had told him it was Hollister who was troubling him, but he hadn't said how or why.

"Willy Hollister," Fat Jack said, with the unmistakable reverence one consummate artist feels for the work of another, "plays ultrafine piano."

A white-vested waiter appeared like a jungle native from around a potted palm, carrying chicory coffee on a silver tray, and deftly placed cups before Nudger and Fat Jack with a gingerness that suggested the dark liquid might explode if spilled.

"Then what's your problem with Hollister?" Nudger asked, sipping the thick, rich brew. He rated it delicious simply on the basis of the aroma, but the taste didn't disappoint. "Didn't you hire him to play his best piano at your club?"

"Hey, there's no problem with his music," Fat Jack said hastily. "Before I go into any detail, Nudger, I gotta know if you'll hang around New Orleans till you can clear up this matter for old Fat Jack." Fat Jack's tiny pinkish eyes glittered with mean humor. "For a fat fee, of course."

Nudger was suspicious of people who referred to themselves in the third person, but he also knew the fee would be generous. Fat Jack had an equally obese bank account, and he had in fact paid a sizable sum for air fare and hotel expenses just for Nudger to travel to New Orleans and sit in the Magnolia Blossom restaurant over lunch and listen to Fat Jack talk. The question Nudger now voiced was, "Why me?"

Fat Jack gave him a broad, flesh-padded grin. "Ain't that the big one of all the whys? The universal question?"

"It is in my universe," Nudger said.

Fat Jack repeated the salient query for Nudger. "Why you? Because I know a lady named Jeanette Boyington from your fair city. Jeanette says you're tops at your job; she don't say that about many."

Nudger almost spilled his coffee. Jeanette Boyington continued to astound, even months after he'd last seen her. And yet he shouldn't have been surprised that the woman who'd tried to dupe him into being her accomplice in murder, who had been virtually destroyed by where their relationship had led him, would recommend him. That was the essential Jeanette Boyington; she was a gamefish who admired persistence above all else. Even from her room in the State Asylum for the Criminally Insane. Nudger wondered if Fat Jack McGee knew Jeanette Boyington's present address.

"And because of your collection," Fat Jack added. An ebony dribble of coffee dangled in tenuous liquid suspension from his triple chin, glittering as he talked. "I mean, I heard you collect old jazz records."

"I used to," Nudger said a bit wistfully, realizing that Fat Jack must have checked him out with some thoroughness. "I had Willie the Lion. Duke Ellington and Mary Lou Williams from their Kansas City days. Bessie Smith. Art Tatum."

"How come 'had'?" Fat Jack asked.

"I sold most of the collection," Nudger said, "to pay the rent one dark month." He gazed beyond green palm fronds, out the window and through filigreed black wrought iron, at the tourists half a block away on Bourbon Street, at the odd combination of French and Spanish architecture and black America and white suits and broiling half-tropical sun that was New Orleans, where jazz lived as in no other place. "Damned rent," he muttered.

"Amen," Fat Jack said solemnly, kidding not even himself. He hadn't worried about paying the rent in years. The drop of coffee released its tremulous grip on his chin, plummeted, and stained his pure white shirtfront like a sacrilege.

Nudger looked away from the stain, back out at Bourbon Street. It had become run down and attracted some of the wrong element—or rather, the *wrong* wrong element—since Nudger had last seen it, but it was still Bourbon Street and like no other street. High notes and low notes; topless and bottomless dancers—male and female; tourists and true jazz lovers. All in a grand and gaudy mix that ran through the heart—that *was* the heart—of the French Quarter. The relatively few violent ones couldn't change that. Tradition had a certain resilience.

"So will you stay around awhile?" Fat Jack was asking.

Nudger nodded. His social and business calendars weren't quite booked solid.

"It's not Hollister himself who worries me," Fat Jack said. "It's Ineida Collins. She's singing at the club now, and if she keeps practicing, someday she'll be mediocre. Hey, I'm not digging at her, Nudger; that's simply an honest assessment of her talent. And talent is a commodity I can judge better than most."

"Then why did you hire her?"

"Because of David Collins. He owns a lot of the French Quarter and a piece of the highly successful restaurant in which we now sit. In every parish in New Orleans, he has more clout than a ton of charge cards. And he's as skinny and ornery as I am fat and nice."

Nudger took another sip of the pungent coffee. "And he asked you to hire Ineida Collins?"

"You're on to it, Nudger. Ineida is his daughter. She wants to make it big as a singer. And she will, even if Daddy has to pay double the fair price for a recording studio. Since David Collins owns the building my club is in, not to mention twelve-and-a-half-percent interest in the business, I thought I'd acquiesce when his daughter auditioned for a job on his recommendation. And Ineida isn't really so bad that she embarrasses anyone but herself, so I call it diplomacy."

"I thought you were calling it trouble," Nudger said. "I thought that was why you hired me."

Fat Jack nodded, ample jowls spilling over his white collar. "So it became," he said. "Hollister is a handsome young dude, and within the first week Ineida was at the club he put some moves on her and they became fast friends, then soon progressed beyond mere friendship."

"You figure he's attracted to Daddy's money?"

"Nothing like that," Fat Jack said. "That'd be too simple. Part of the deal when I hired Ineida was that I keep her identity a secret—David Collins insisted on it. She wants to stand or fall alone; all that making-it-on-her-own bullshit. So she sings under the stage name of Ineida Mann, which most likely is a gem from her dad's advertising department. It doesn't make it any easier for me to be her guardian angel."

"I still don't see your problem," Nudger said.

"Hollister doesn't set right with me, and I don't know exactly why. I do know that if he messes up Ineida in some way, David Collins will see to it that I'm playing jazz at clubs on the Butte, Boise, Anchorage circuit."

"Nice cities in their fashion," Nudger remarked, "but not jazz towns. I see your problem."

"So find out about Willy Hollister for me," Fat Jack implored. "Check him out, declare him pass or fail, but put my mind at ease either way. Hey, that's all I want, an easeful mind."

"Even we tough private eye guys want that," Nudger said.

Fat Jack removed his napkin from his lap and raised a languid plump hand. A waiter who had been born just to respond to that signal scampered over with the check. Fat Jack accepted a tiny ballpoint pen and signed for the meal with a ponderous yet elegant flourish. Nudger watched him help himself to a mint. It was like watching the grace and dexterity of an elephant picking up a peanut. Huge as Fat Jack was, he moved as if he weighed no more than ten or twelve pounds.

"I gotta get back, Nudger, do some paperwork, count some money." He stood up, surprisingly tall in his tan slacks and white linen sport coat. Nudger thought it was a sharp-looking coat; he decided he might buy one and wear it winter and summer. "Drop around the club about eight o'clock tonight," Fat Jack said. "I'll fill you in on whatever else you need to know, and I'll point out Willy Hollister and Ineida. Maybe you'll get to hear her sing."

"While she's singing," Nudger said, "maybe we can discuss my fee."

Fat Jack grinned, his vast jowls defying gravity grandly. "Hey, you and me'll get along fine." He winked and moved away among the tables, tacking toward the door.

The waiter refilled Nudger's coffee cup, and he sat sipping chicory brew and watching Fat Jack McGee move along the sunny sidewalk toward Bourbon Street. He sure had a bouncy, jaunty kind of walk for a fat man.

Nudger wasn't as anxious about the fee as Fat Jack thought. Well, not quite as anxious; he knew he'd be paid for his work. The reason he'd jumped at the case wasn't totally because of the fee, even though he desperately needed something to toss to Eileen and the various wolves queued up at his door. Years ago, at the Odds Against lounge in St. Louis, Nudger had heard Fat Jack McGee play clarinet in the manner that had made him a jazz legend, and he'd never forgotten. Fat Jack's was the kind of music that lingered in the mind, that you thought of at odd moments: while you were waiting in a doorway for the rain to stop, or sitting on the edge of the bed tying your shoe. It was music that permeated dreams, that hooked real jazz fans forever.

Nudger needed the money, sure. But he also needed to hear that clarinet again.

III

Fat Jack's club was on Conti, a few blocks off Bourbon Street. Nudger paused at the entrance and looked up at a red-and-green neon sign that visually shouted the synonymous names of club and owner. And there was a red neon Fat Jack himself, a portly, herky-jerky illuminated figure that jumped about with the same seeming lightness and jauntiness as the flesh-and-blood version.

A trumpet solo from inside the club was wafting out almost palpably into the hot, syrupy-humid night. People came and went, among them a few who were obviously tourists making the Bourbon Street rounds of clubs and drinks. But Nudger got the impression that most of Fat Jack's customers were folks who took their jazz seriously and were there for music and not atmosphere.

The trumpet stair-stepped up to an admirable high C and wild applause. Nudger went inside and looked around.

Dim, smoky, lots of people at lots of tables. Men in suits and in jeans and T-shirts; women in long dresses and casual slacks. The small stage was empty now; the band was between sets. Customers milled around, stacking up at the long bar along one wall. Waitresses in black, red-lettered "Fat Jack's" T-shirts bustled about with trays of drinks. Near the left of the stage was a polished dark upright piano that gleamed like a showroom-new car even in the dimness. Nudger decided that Fat Jack's was everything a jazz club should be.

Feeling that his heart was home, he made his way to the bar and, after a five-minute wait, ordered a mug of draft beer. The mug was frosted, the beer ice-flecked. Nudger was glad, right now, that he'd agreed to work for Fat Jack.

"Ain't no ten-dollar bill," said a deep, velvety voice just down the bar from Nudger, "I gave you a twenty."

"Sorry, sir, it was a ten."

Nudger leaned forward and saw that the deep voice belonged to a tall, lanky black man with wide shoulders, a scraggly goatee, and large, splay-fingered hands that looked strong enough to be leased out to industry. The "Sorry, sir" belonged to the bartender, who didn't appear old enough to be working where liquor was served, but whose dark eyes had a wise and steady gunfighter calm about them.

"You tryin' to pull some shit on me!" the black man said. He was working himself up to high pitch. Around him, the other customers let their conversations taper off to nervous silence. "You owe me change from a twenty, clown, and you gonna pay!"

The bartender with the high-school face and been-around eyes said nothing, didn't move. He did, however, smile slightly.

"I'll give you a jive-ass smile under your chin!" the black guy said. He reached out with his big right hand to grip the bartender's shirtfront, but the bartender took an easy step back, using the bar to shield him from harm. The big man's other huge hand slid beneath the leather vest he was wearing over his red shirt, as if to pull out a knife to make good his threat of a tracheal grin.

The bartender said, "Marty." Not in a scared voice, but as if he could handle things himself—just that oversized homicidal customers simply weren't part of his job; something in the union rules.

Marty was already there. He was a medium-sized, bland-faced man in a brown suit that matched his straight, brown, razor-styled hair. Mr. Average, with a Sears-catalog look about him.

Marty's hand snapped in a blur to the big man's thick wrist. The abrupt, smooth movement reminded Nudger of a snake striking. Marty smiled in a kindly fashion while the large black face above him registered outrage, then surprise at the absence of fear in the smaller, bland white man and the strength of the fingers about his wrist. Some average. The big man calmed down, withdrawing the hand from inside the leather vest as Marty loosened his grip by degrees.

"He did me outa my twenty," the man said, gesturing with his head toward the bartender. He was still plenty mad, still unpredictable and dangerous. But his outrage had lost its edge.

"Are you sure of that, sir?" Marty asked.

"Sheeit, yeah, I'm sure!"

"So let's talk about it," Marty said, further defusing the situation. "What are you drinking?"

The man scratched his patchy beard. "Uh, vodka with a twist."

Marty nodded to the bartender, who poured two generous vodkas over ice and set them on the bar.

"On the house," Marty said, picking up both drinks and leading the way to a corner table, not glancing back.

The big man looked uncertain for a few seconds. Then, glad for a way out of the confrontation without losing his machismo, he followed Marty and the vodka across the crowded floor.

They sat down and began talking quietly. The black man leaned his long body forward over the table, speaking earnestly, sensing he'd found an impartial ear. Nudger knew that sooner or later Marty would give him the extra ten in his change as a gesture of goodwill and good business, not to mention keeping the bartender alive.

Conversation picked up again around the bar. Nudger lifted his beer mug and sipped. He wanted to ask the bartender who Marty was, but the unflappable young man was working the other end of the bar for a group of middle-aged women ordering exotic drinks topped with pineapple slices and little paper parasols.

The lights brightened and dimmed three times, apparently a signal the regulars at Fat Jack's understood, for they gradually began a general movement back toward their tables.

Then the lights dimmed considerably, and the stage, with its gleaming piano, was suddenly the only illuminated area in the place. A tall, graceful man in his thirties walked onstage to the kind of scattered but enthusiastic applause that suggests a respect and a common bond between performer and audience.

The man smiled faintly at the applause and sat down at the piano. He had pained, haughty features, blond hair that curled above the collar of his black Fat Jack's T-shirt. He was thin, but the muscles in his bare arms were corded; his hands appeared elegant yet very strong. This was Willy Hollister, the main gig, starbound but still their own, the one the paying customers had come to hear. The place got quiet and he began to play.

The song was a variation of "Good Woman Gone Bad," an old number originally written for tenor sax. Hollister played it his way, and two bars into it Nudger knew he was better than good and nothing but bad luck could keep him from becoming great. He was backed by brass and a snare drum, but he didn't need it; he didn't need a thing in this world but that piano and you could tell it just by looking at the rapt expression on his aristocratic face. He wasn't playing the music; he *was* the music.

"Didn't I tell you it was all there?" Fat Jack said softly beside Nudger. "Whatever else there is about him, the man can play piano."

Nudger nodded silently in agreement. Jazz basically is black music, but the fair, blond Hollister played it with all the soul and pain of its genesis. He finished the number to riotous applause that quieted only when he swung into another, a blues piece. He sang this one while his hands worked the piano. His voice was as black as his music; in his tone, his inflection, there seemed to dwell echoes of centuries of suffering.

"I'm impressed," Nudger said, when the applause for the blues number had died down.

"You and everyone else with ears," Fat Jack said, sipping absinthe from a gold-rimmed glass. "Hollister won't be playing here much longer before moving up the show-business ladder—not for what I'm paying him, and I'm paying him plenty."

"How did you happen to hire him?"

"He came recommended by a club owner in Chicago. Seems he started out in Cleveland playing small rooms, then moved up to better things in Kansas City and your town, St. Louis, then Rush Street in Chicago. All I had to do was hear him play for five minutes to know I wanted to hire him. It's like catching a Ray Charles or a Garner on the way up. The man's an original."

Nudger didn't remember Hollister ever playing St. Louis, but that wasn't surprising. Nudger hadn't listened to live jazz in years, and not much recorded jazz since his collection had been ravaged by incensed creditors. Diluted FM radio music had comprised most of his listening lately. The stuff of elevators.

"So what specifically is there about Hollister that bothers you?" Nudger asked. "Why shouldn't he be seeing Ineida Collins?"

Fat Jack scrunched up his padded features, seeking the word that might convey the thought. "His music is . . . uneven."

"That's hardly a crime," Nudger said, "especially if he can play so well when he's right."

"He ain't as right as I've heard him," Fat Jack said. "Believe me, Hollister can be even better than he is tonight. But it's not really his music that concerns me. Hollister acts weird sometimes, secretive. Sam Judman, the drummer, went by his apartment last week, found the door unlocked and let himself in to wait for Hollister to get home. So what happens? When Hollister discovers him there he beats up on Sam—with his fists. Can you imagine a piano player like Hollister using his hands for *that*?" Fat Jack looked as if he'd discovered a hair in his absinthe. "He warned Judman never to snoop around his apartment again. I mean, talked hard to the man!"

"So he's obsessively secretive," Nudger said. "I still don't see why you need me." What am I doing, he asked himself, trying to talk myself out of a job? What would Eileen think if she could hear me? What would her shark of a lawyer think? Blood in the water.

But Fat Jack said, "Hey, believe me, I need you. Hollister has been troubled, jumpy, and unpredictable, for the last month. He's got problems, and he's seeing Ineida Collins, so I got problems. I figure it'd be wise to learn some more about Willy Hollister."

"I understand," Nudger said. "The better to know if his intentions toward the lady are honorable, as they used to say."

"And in some quarters still do," Fat Jack pointed out. "Only they don't fight duels over those matters around here anymore; in a duel both parties have a chance. What we see now are mostly one shot affairs, usually in somebody's back."

Nudger felt a cold twinge of fear. He didn't like murder; he didn't even like talking about murder.

"Are you afraid David Collins might shoot you?" he asked.

Fat Jack lifted the massive shoulders inside his pale jacket. "Naw, I guess not. What I'm afraid of is he'll see to it that I wanna shoot myself."

Nudger wasn't totally reassured. Nobody could exude fear like a fat man, and fear seemed to live and feed inside Fat Jack like a malignant overmatched tapeworm.

"Who's Marty?" Nudger asked, looking around but not seeing the brown-suited man who'd so skillfully handled trouble earlier in the evening.

"Marty Sievers," Fat Jack said. "He's my floor manager."

"You mean bouncer?"

"Naw. Marty's in charge when I'm not here. And we don't need a bouncer with him around. He's ex-Green Beret.

Black belt, all that mean stuff. But he don't use it if he don't have to."

"The ones who really have it usually are that way," Nudger said.

"I guess. You know any martial arts? A guy in your business should."

"I'm yellow belt," Nudger said, "only mine runs vertically, up the back."

"Huh?"

"Never mind. Have you talked to Marty about Hollister?"

"Some. Not much. I asked him to keep an eye on the situation, keep me clued in on anything that happens between Ineida and Hollister that I should know about. Marty's too busy running the place to see much else, though. He's got enough of a job keeping watch on the liquor and seeing the help don't dip into the till."

The lights did their three-time dimming routine again, the crowd quieted, and Willy Hollister was back at the piano. But this time the center of attention was the tall dark-haired girl leaning with one hand on the piano, her other hand delicately holding a microphone as if the heat from her fingertips might melt it. Inside her plain navy-blue dress was a trim figure. She had nice ankles, a nice smile, nice eyes. Nice was a word that might have been coined just for her. A stage name like Ineida Mann didn't fit her at all. She was prom queen and Girl Scouts and PTA and looked as if she'd blush fire-engine red at an off-color joke. But maybe all of that was simply a role; maybe she was playing for contrast. Showbiz types were good at that.

Fat Jack knew what Nudger was thinking. "She's as straight and naive as she looks," he said. "But she'd like to be something else, to learn all about life and love in a few easy lessons. You know how some young rich girls are."

Nudger knew. "Is Hollister the guy to teach her?"

"You might think so, judging by his surface qualities, but I think he might be a phony. I think he might take her straight through to graduation, but no diploma. And that's what scares me enough to hire you."

Someone in the backup band announced Ineida Mann. There was light applause, and she acknowledged it with a smile, slipped into the pensive mood of the music, and began to sing the plaintive lyrics of an old blues standard. She had control but no range. Nudger found himself listening to the backup music, which included a smooth clarinet.

The band liked Ineida and went all out to envelope her in good sound, but the audience at Fat Jack's was too smart for that. Ineida finished to more light applause, bowed prettily, and made her exit. Competent but nothing special, and looking as if she'd just wandered in from suburbia. But this was what she wanted and her rich father was getting it for her. Parental love could be as blind as the other kind. Sometimes it could cause just as much trouble.

The lights came on full brightness, and conversation and the sale of drinks stepped up in volume and activity. There apparently would be no more music for a while. Some of the customers began drifting toward the door, to continue roaming the night for more fun or blues or whatever else they needed. It was early yet; there was promise in the air.

"The crowd'll thin out soon," Fat Jack said. "It's Hollister they came to hear."

"They stuck around for Ineida's act."

"Jazz folks are a polite audience. And like I told you, Ineida ain't all that bad. She's worth the cover price, once the customers are in. But it's people like Hollister that get them in." Fat Jack took another delicate sip of his absinthe, diamond ring and gold bracelet flashing in the dimness. "So how are you going to get started on this thing, Nudger? You want me to introduce you to Hollister and Ineida? Or are you gonna sneak around sleuth-style?"

"Usually I begin a case by discussing my fee and signing a contract," Nudger said.

Fat Jack waved his immaculately manicured, jewel-adorned hand. "Hey, don't worry about fee. Let's make it whatever you usually charge plus twenty percent plus expenses. Trust me on that."

That sounded fine to Nudger, all except the trusting part. He reached into his inside coat pocket, withdrew his roll of antacid tablets, thumbed back the aluminum foil, and popped one of the white disks into his mouth, all in one practiced smooth motion.

"What's that stuff for?" Fat Jack asked.

"Nervous stomach."

"You oughta try this," Fat Jack said, nodding toward his absinthe. "Eventually it eliminates the stomach altogether."

Nudger winced, feeling his abdomen twitch. "I want to talk with Ineida," he said, "but it would be best if we had our conversation away from the club. And without us having been introduced."

Fat Jack pursed his lips thoughtfully and nodded. He said, "I can give you her address. She doesn't live at home with her father; she's in a little apartment over on Beulah Street. It's all part of the making-it-on-her-own illusion. I can give you Hollister's address, too."

"Fine."

"Anything else?"

"Maybe. Do you still play the clarinet?"

"Does Andy Williams still sing 'Moon River'?"

Nudger smiled. A silly question deserved a silly question. Fat Jack cocked his head and looked curiously at

Nudger, one tiny eye squinting through the tobacco smoke that hazed the air around the bar. "The truth is, I only play now and then, on special occasions. You aren't going to ask me to play at your wedding, are you?"

"It's too late for that," Nudger said, "but a blues number would have been perfect on that occasion. Why don't we make my price for this job my usual fee plus only ten percent plus you do a set with the clarinet here some Saturday night?"

Fat Jack beamed, then threw back his head and let out a roaring laugh that drew stares and seemed to rattle the bottles on the backbar. "Agreed! You're a find, Nudger! First you trust me to pay you without a contract, then you lower your fee and ask for a clarinet solo instead of money. Hey, there's no place you can spend a clarinet solo! I like you, but you're not much of a businessman."

Nudger kept a straight face and sipped his beer. Fat Jack hadn't bothered to find out the amount of Nudger's usual fee, so all this talk about percentages meant nothing. If detectives weren't good businessmen, neither were jazz musicians. He handed Fat Jack a pen and a club matchbook. "How about those addresses?"

Still smiling expansively, Fat Jack flipped back the matchbook cover and wrote.

IV

Beulah Street was narrow and crooked, lined with low houses of French-Spanish architecture. It was an array of arches, ornate shutters, pastel stucco, and ornamental wrought iron and wood scrollwork. The houses long ago had been divided into apartments, each with a separate entrance. Behind each apartment was a small courtyard. A behemoth street-cleaning machine was roaring and hissing along the opposite curb at about three miles per hour, laboring as if its bulk were being dragged forward only by the rotating motion of its heavy-bristled disk brush digging against the curb. Nudger moved well over on the sidewalk so he wouldn't catch any of the spray from the water jetted out in front of the determinedly rotating brush.

He found Ineida Collins' address in the middle of the block. It belonged to a pale yellow structure with a weathered tile roof and a riot of multicolored bougainvillea blooming wild halfway up one cracked and much-patched stucco wall. Harsh sunlight washed half the wall in purifying brilliance; the other half was in deep shadow.

Nudger glanced at his wristwatch. Ten o'clock. Ineida might still be in bed. If the street-cleaning machine hadn't awakened her, he would. He stepped up onto the small red brick front porch and worked the lion's-head knocker on a plank door supported by huge black iron hinges pocked with rust. A fat honeybee buzzed lazily over from the bougainvillea to see what all the fuss was about.

Ineida came to the door without much delay, fully dressed in black slacks and a peach-colored silky blouse. She didn't appear at all sleepy after her late-night stint at Fat Jack's. Her dark hair was tied back in a French braid. Even the cruel sunlight was kind to her; she looked young, and as innocent and naive as Fat Jack said she was. A Brothers Grimm princess with the money to live the fairy tale.

Nudger smiled and told her he was a writer doing a piece on Fat Jack's club. "I heard you sing last night," he said, before she could question his identification. "It really was something to see. I thought it might be a good idea if we talked."

It was impossible for her to turn down what in her mind was a celebrity interview. The Big Break might arrive anytime from any source. She lit up brightly, even in the brilliant sunlight, and invited Nudger inside.

Her apartment was tastefully but inexpensively furnished; she really was living independently away from Daddy. There was an imitation oriental rug on the hardwood floor, lots of rattan furniture, a Casablanca ceiling fan rotating its wide flat blades slowly, not moving air but casting soothing flickering shadows. Through sheer beige curtains the apartment's courtyard was visible, well tended and colorful. A subtle sweet scent hung in the still air, either a trace of incense or from something growing in the courtyard garden. Some pale blue stationery and a pen lay on a small desk; Ineida had been preparing to write a letter.

"Can I get you a cup of coffee, Mr. Nudger?" she asked.

Nudger told her yes, thanks, then watched the sway of her trim hips as she walked into the small kitchen. From where he sat he could see a Mr. Coffee brewer on the sink, its glass pot half full. He watched Ineida pour, then return with two cups of coffee. She asked Nudger if he wanted cream or sugar and he declined.

He asked, "How old are you, Ineida?"

"Twenty-two." She placed his coffee on the table next to him.

"Young enough not to have to lie about your age," he said.

Her smile was forced. "I wish I were older."

"You'll change your mind about that," Nudger said. "Everybody does. You can't have sung professionally for very long."

She sat down, centering her steaming cup on a coaster. "About four years, actually. I sang in school productions, then studied for a while in New York. I've been singing at Fat Jack's for about two months. I love it."

"And the crowd seems to love you," Nudger fibbed. He watched her smile and figured the lie was a worthy one. There was a vulnerability about her that needed protecting. Certain men might view it as something to exploit. Not Nudger. No, siree!

He pretended to take notes while he asked her a string of writerlike questions, pumping up her ego. It was an ego that would inflate only so far. Nudger decided that he liked Ineida Collins and hoped she would hurry up and realize she wasn't Ineida Mann.

The street cleaner roared past again, snailing along in the opposite direction to tidy up the near curb. Nudger could hear its coarse brush scraping on the pavement. He sat quietly, waiting patiently for the monster to pass.

"I'm told that you and Willy Hollister, the piano player, are pretty good friends," he said, in the converging quiet.

Ineida's mood changed abruptly. Suspicion crept into her dark eyes. The youthful, smiling mouth became taut and suddenly ten years older. It was a preview of what she would be after life had fallen on her.

"You're not a magazine writer," she said in a betrayed voice.

Nudger felt guilty about deceiving her, as if he'd tried to lure her into a car with candy. "No, I'm not," he admitted. His stomach gave a mulelike kick. What a profession he'd stumbled into!

"Then who are you?"

"Someone concerned about your well-being."

She narrowed her eyes at him. Her smooth chin jutted forward in a way that suggested more than a mere streak of obstinacy. Nudger caught a glimpse of why Fat Jack saw her as trouble.

Antacid time. He popped one of the chalky white disks into his mouth and chewed. The sound of it breaking up was surprisingly loud.

"Father sent you," she said.

"No," Nudger said. Chomp, chomp.

"Liar!" She stood up and flounced to the door. She did a terrific flounce. "Get out," she said.

"I'd like to talk with you about Willy Hollister," Nudger persisted. He knew that in his business persistence paid one way or the other. He could only hope that this time it wouldn't be the other.

"Get out," Ineida repeated. "Or I'll call the police. Better yet, I'll scream for them. Right here with the door open."

Scream? Police?

Within ten seconds Nudger was outside again on Beulah Street, staring at the uncompromising barrier of Ineida's closed door. Apparently she was touchy on the subject of Willy Hollister. Nudger slipped another antacid tablet between his lips. He turned his back to the warming sun and began walking, keeping to the dry half of the sidewalk, away from the curb.

He'd gone half a block when he realized that he was casting three shadows. He stopped. The middle shadow stopped also, but the larger ones on either side kept advancing. The large bodies that cast those shadows were suddenly standing in front of Nudger. Two very big men were staring down at him—one was smiling, one not. Considering the kind of smile it was, that didn't make much difference.

"We noticed you talking to Miss Mann," the one on the left said. He had a black mustache, wide cheekbones, dark, pockmarked skin, and gray eyes that gave no quarter. "Whatever you said to her seemed to upset her." His accent was a cross between a Southern drawl and clipped French. Nudger recognized it as Cajun. The Cajuns were a tough, predominantly French people who had settled southern Louisiana but never themselves.

Nudger allowed himself to hope the large men's interest in him was passing and started to walk on. The second man, who was shorter but had a massive neck and shoulders, glided on shuffling feet like a heavyweight boxer to block his way. Nudger swallowed his antacid tablet.

"You nervous, my friend?" the boxer asked in the same rich accent.

"Habitually," Nudger managed to answer in a choked voice.

Pockmarked said, "We have an interest in Miss Mann's welfare. What were you talking to her about?"

"The conversation was private." Nudger's stomach was on spin cycle. "Do you two fellows mind introducing yourselves?"

"We mind," the boxer said. He was smiling again. God, it was a nasty smile. Nudger noticed that the tip of the man's right eyebrow had turned dead white where it was crossed by a thin scar.

"Then I'm sorry, but we have nothing to talk about."

Pockmarked shook his head patiently in disagreement. "We have this to talk about, my friend. There are parts of this great state of Looziahna that are vast swampland. Not far from where we stand, the bayou is wild and the home of a surprising number of alligators. People go into the bayou, and some of them never come out. Who knows about them? After a while, who cares?" The cold gray eyes had diamond chips in them. "You understand my meaning?"

Nudger nodded. He understood. His stomach understood.

"I think we've made ourselves clear," Pockmarked said. "We aren't nice men, sir. It's our business not to be nice, and it's our pleasure. So a man like yourself, sir, a reasonable man in good health, should listen to us and stay away from Miss Mann."

"You mean Miss Collins."

"I mean Miss Ineida Mann." He said it with the straight face of a true professional.

"Why don't you tell Willy Hollister to stay away from her?" Nudger asked. Some of his fear had left him now, supplanted by a curiosity of the kind that killed the cat.

"Mr. Hollister is a nice young man of Miss Mann's own

choosing," Pockmarked said with an odd courtliness. "You she obviously doesn't like. You upset her. That upsets us."

"And me and Frick don't like to be upset," the boxer said. He closed a powerful hand on the lapel of Nudger's sport jacket, not pushing or pulling in the slightest, merely squeezing the material. Nudger could feel the vibrant force of the man's strength, as if it were electric current. "Behave yourself," the boxer hissed through his fixed smile.

He abruptly released his grip, and both men turned and walked away.

Nudger looked down at his abused lapel. It was as crimped as if it had been set wrinkled in a vise for days. He wondered if the dry cleaners could do anything about it when they pressed the coat.

Then he realized he was shaking. He loathed danger and had no taste for violence. He needed another antacid tablet and then, even though it was early, a drink.

New Orleans promised to be an exciting city, but not in the way the travel agencies and Chamber of Commerce advertised.

V

Nudger considered phoning Sam Judman to make sure he was home before dropping by to see him. Then he decided against calling. It would be better to talk to Judman without giving the drummer time to prepare for the conversation. The element of surprise would increase the chances that Judman, possibly still angry from being beaten by Hollister, would say something accidentally that might provide some insight into what was causing Fat Jack to worry.

Judman lived in a crumbling brick building in the French Quarter, in a spacious old second-floor apartment that was lined with screened windows. He was a small, intense, dark-haired man, in his early forties, with a narrow, lined face and an underlying pallor that suggested ill health. He was unmarked; there was no longer any sign of the beating at Hollister's hands. When Nudger introduced himself and asked to talk about Hollister, Judman nodded and invited him inside.

The apartment was cool after the noontime heat. Four large ceiling fans rotated slowly in unison, and all of the windows were open. One of the fans was making a faint rhythmic ticking sound, a lazy summer sound. Bamboo blinds were lowered exactly halfway down all the way around the spacious single room, their horizontal precision making the place seem even larger than it was. There were a few pieces of modern but comfortable-looking furniture. Books, record albums, and tapes lined one wall. Framed and glassed photos of Judman posed with various show-business personalities were hung in the narrow space above the windows, picking up reflections. The room was very bright where it was bright, very dark where the sun failed to penetrate. A door led to what appeared to be a small space for a drop-down Murphy bed; through another door Nudger could see into a kitchen. In the far corner near that door was a multi-million-dollar stereo setup.

Judman offered to get Nudger something to drink. Nudger had already had his day's ration of liquor, and coffee would send his stomach into acidic revolt. He declined Judman's offer and the two men sat facing each other in low-slung, plushly padded matching chairs.

"You said you were a private detective, Mr. Nudger," Judman said. "May I ask the identity of your client?"

"Right now," Nudger said, "I'd prefer to keep that confidential."

"But you want to know about Willy Hollister."

"Whatever you can tell me. I know you and he had a run-in at his apartment. Do you know why?"

Judman turned his hands palms-up in a perplexed gesture and then dropped them to his knees. "He was upset because I let myself in to wait for him. I don't know why he was so touchy; he'd left the door unlocked. And it's not as if I was going through the drawers or testing for dust. I was just sitting on the couch waiting for him to show up after work. I didn't figure the guy was paranoid."

"How long had you been there before Hollister arrived?"

"Not more than five minutes. Hell, I told him that, but it didn't seem to make any difference. He was in a freaked-out rage."

There was a noise from the kitchen. Nudger turned.

Marty Sievers walked in, carrying a tall glass of dark liquid with ice in it. When he got closer, Nudger realized it was iced coffee. Nudger stood and shook hands with Sievers, who didn't seem surprised to see him.

"I know who you are," Sievers said. "I saw you at the club last night, and I heard you introduce yourself to Sam."

Nudger was sure there was little that Sievers' bland brown eyes missed. Sievers sipped his iced coffee; he had about him the stillness and control of a man who had supreme confidence in his physical capabilities in any situation. Green Beret stuff.

"You handled that potential customer trouble very neatly last night at the club," Nudger said.

Sievers swirled the ice in his glass. "It's part of my job."

"You're wondering why Marty's here," Sam Judman said.

Nudger nodded, "My line of work, wondering."

"And finding answers," Sievers added. "I'll make it easy this time. I came here to tell Sam about some leads with other clubs around town."

"Leads?"

"Employment opportunities."

Nudger looked at Judman. "You're leaving the band at Fat Jack's?"

A passing anger momentarily darkened the drummer's pale features. "Not voluntarily. Fat Jack let me go, after my fight with Hollister."

"He had to," Sievers said, shrugging.

Judman nodded in reluctant understanding. "Yeah, Hollister saw to that, told Fat Jack it was me or him. Hollister's a bastard, but I have to admit I'm easier to replace than he is. This is a jazz town, full of top musicians looking to latch on someplace."

"It's a raw deal," Sievers said. "Fat Jack and I want to see that Sam lands on his feet." He carried his drink to a flowered sofa, sat down in a corner, and became as relaxed and motionless as a wax-museum display. He was like an actor doing an upstage freeze, turning the scene over to Nudger and Sam Judman.

"Why did you go to see Hollister the day you had the fight?" Nudger asked Judman.

"No reason out of the ordinary. I had a few suggestions on the arrangement of one of Hollister's numbers. I wanted to change the background beat."

"Does Hollister do his own arranging?"

"Yep," Judman said. "He does everything. And even though he cost me my job, I gotta say he does it well."

"So how come he got so excited when he came home and saw you in his apartment? Did he act as if he had something to hide?"

"What he acted like was mad. He didn't give me a chance to explain why I was there, just started in on me with his fists. And he didn't explain to me why he didn't want me there."

"Is he dealing in drugs?" Nudger asked.

"No," Sievers said definitely from the corner of the couch.

"A user?" Nudger asked.

"Sure," Judman said. "Nothing hard, though, a little coke, a little good grass now and then. Means nothing."

"Did he apologize or try to patch things up after the fight?"

Judman laughed. "Apologize? Not Hollister."

"And he didn't tell you or anyone else why he beat up on you?"

"When I asked him the next day," Judman said, "all he'd say was that he didn't like his privacy invaded."

"Maybe that's all there is to it," Sievers suggested.

"Maybe," Nudger agreed, not believing it. "What do you know about Hollister and Ineida Mann?" he asked Judman.

"Only that they're chummy. Ineida seems like a nice kid; she don't deserve Hollister."

"What do you think of her as a performer?"

"A nice kid."

Nudger looked over and saw that Sievers' bland face was as unreadable as a turnip. He wondered if Sievers knew that Ineida Mann was the daughter of David Collins. That was one he'd have to ask Fat Jack.

"If Fat Jack fired you," Nudger said to Judman, "then Hollister doesn't carry his own backup band."

"That's right," Judman said. "The club uses its own backup music; I've been playing there a couple of years."

"It won't be long before Hollister takes his own musicians wherever he plays," Sievers said. "They'll line up for the job. He's that good."

Nudger looked at Judman. "Do you think he's that good? A rising star?"

"Star? The son of a bitch is a meteor." He didn't like saying it, but he got the words out at a cost. Dean Martin, his arm flung around Judman's shoulders, smiled down approvingly from an eight-by-ten glossy.

"Meteors are bright," Nudger said, "but they travel in a downward direction and burn out fast."

Judman grinned at the thought, but said, "I'm no astronomer, Nudger. I bang the drums."

Nudger stood up and thanked Judman for taking the time to talk with him.

"No problem," the drummer said, getting up to show Nudger out. "I figure to have plenty of free time for a while."

"Not for long," Sievers said, also standing. "You're too good a musician not to catch on somewhere soon. I'll leave with you, Nudger." He gave Judman a reassuring smile. "Let me know about those auditions we set up over on Rampart."

"I will, Mr. Sievers. And thanks again."

At the door, Judman shook hands with Sievers, then Nudger. His eyes were weary and his hand felt cold and weak.

Sievers fell in step beside Nudger as they walked along the crooked sidewalks of St. Philip. "I wanted to talk to you alone," he told Nudger. "Fat Jack hired you." He stated it as a fact, not a question.

"Did he tell you that?" Nudger asked.

"No. I saw the way you and he were talking last night at the club. And I know he's plenty worried."

"About what?"

"We both know what. Or rather who. Willy Hollister."

"Do you think he's got good reason to worry?"

Sievers walked silently for a while before answering, his heels striking a soft rhythm on the sidewalk. "I'm not sure. The more you see of Hollister, the less you like him. Fat Jack tells me there's something uneven about his music, but you couldn't prove it by me. I only judge him by the number of customers he draws, and that seems constant. I'm tone deaf. It all sounds like 'The Star-Spangled Banner' to me, even Hollister's music."

"What about Hollister and Ineida?"

"They're lovers," Sievers said. "That's no secret. What's their personal life got to do with anything?"

"I don't know," Nudger said. "I'm still trying to get a slant on things, find a toehold."

"Why specifically did Fat Jack hire you?" Sievers asked flatly.

"Maybe you better ask him."

"Sure, I will." Sievers didn't seem at all miffed by Nudger's refusal to answer. This was a man who never wasted anger.

"What exactly is your business relationship with Fat Jack?" Nudger asked. "I get the impression you're more than simply an employee." He smiled. "If you'd prefer, I'll ask Fat Jack."

Sievers laughed. "No, that's okay, I'll tell you. I'm a minority partner in the club—technically, we've got a limited partnership. But mainly I'm the floor manager. I keep the place running smoothly, do most of the hiring and firing, the procurement of supplies. Fat Jack hires the musical talent, does the paperwork, and reaps most of the profit. I get a salary and a percentage of the net."

"How do you like that arrangement?"

"Fine. It's what we agreed on from the beginning. Fat Jack put up most of the seed money for the club, took most of the risk. Neither of us can bitch. We're both doing okay financially."

"David Collins owns a piece of the club too, doesn't he?"

"Right. Twelve and a half percent, just like me. Only he doesn't need the money."

"Are there any other minority partners?"

"Nope, the other seventy-five percent is all Fat Jack's."

"You were career military, weren't you?" Nudger asked.

"Does it show that much?"

"It does. But I know because Fat Jack told me. You were Green Beret."

"That's right. Vietnam and seven years after that."

"How come you gave it up?"

"It was fine in the beginning, but I got tired of playing games."

"Games?"

"That's right, Nudger. The kinds of wars we're fighting these days are bloody and tragic, but they're nothing more than games played by politicians, with too many rules and restrictions. Wars should be fought only when there's no other way, and they should be fought with all-out effort; you survive or the enemy survives. Wars shouldn't be anybody's games, played with guns without bullets."

"How did you get involved with Fat Jack?"

"When I left the service, I came here because it's my hometown. My wife and I lived here before our divorce, a long time ago. I was a construction foreman for a while, up around Lake Pontchartrain. Then the building industry went bust, and I started doing some serious investing in the stock market—gambling, really—with some of the army severance money I had left. Fat Jack and I were in the same investment club. We got to know each other, thought the same way about certain investments. When I heard he was going to open his own jazz club, I wanted in. We talked, and then made the arrangements."

"What kind of investment club were you in?" Nudger asked.

"One of those deals where the members pool their funds to purchase large blocks of stock or real estate partnerships. It fell apart several years ago when the stock market went into a swoon."

"You must know most of the backup musicians at the club," Nudger said.

"Sure. I know them all."

"What do they think of Willy Hollister?"

"As a talent, they think he's God. As a person they don't particularly like him, but that doesn't bother them much. Or him. They know they're staying put, and he's heading for Grammy awards, Mount Olympus, and the David Letterman show."

"Has he had trouble with any of the other musicians?"

"No, only Judman." Sievers' voice became serious. "It's a good thing he didn't break any bones."

"Judman seems okay."

"I didn't mean Judman," Sievers said, mildly surprised, "I meant Willy Hollister. He used his fists. He might have fractured a knuckle and been unable to play piano."

"And that would cost the club," Nudger said.

"That's right. Hollister packs in the paying customers and helps fatten my bank account."

"Heartless capitalist," Nudger said, only half joking.

"I've got a heart," Sievers said with a grin. "It just happens to be stony and cold." They'd reached an intersection. "You going to the club?"

"No," Nudger said, "my hotel. It's the other way."

"Okay," Sievers said. "I guess I'll see you at the club later."

"You will," Nudger told him, and watched him walk away. Sievers walked with a measured, smooth military erectness that, from a distance, made him appear much taller than he was. It was a walk that suggested control and efficiency. As he reached the next corner, the traffic light seemed to change just for him, and he crossed the intersection without breaking stride.

Probably, Nudger thought, he was humming any number of tunes, all of which were "The Star-Spangled Banner."

VI

You're no jazz-magazine writer," Willy Hollister said to Nudger, in a small back room of Fat Jack's club. It wasn't exactly a dressing room, though at times it served as such. It was a sort of all-purpose place where quick costume changes were made and breaks were taken between sets. The room's pale green paint was faded and peeling, and a steam pipe jutted from floor to ceiling against one wall. Halfway up the pipe was a large paint-caked valve handle that looked as if it hadn't been turned in decades. Yellowed show posters featuring jazz greats were taped here and there on the walls behind the odd assortment of worn furniture. Duke Ellington, Bessie Smith, Billie Holiday, Louis Armstrong. The room was filled with the mingled scents of stale booze and tobacco smoke.

"But I *am* a jazz fan," Nudger said. "Enough of one to know how good you are, and that you play piano in a way that wasn't self-taught." He smiled. "I'll bet you can even read music."

"You have to read music," Hollister said haughtily, "to graduate from the Juilliard School of Music."

Impressive. Even Nudger knew that Juilliard graduates weren't slouches. You had to be able to whistle Beethoven's Fifth all the way through even to get into the place. "So you have a classical-music background," he said to Hollister.

Hollister shrugged. "That's nothing rare; lots of jazz musicians have classical-music roots. You oughta know that, jazz man that you claim to be."

Nudger studied Hollister as the pianist spoke. Offstage he appeared older. His blond hair was thinning on top and his features were losing their boyishness, becoming craggy. His complexion had an unhealthy nicotine-stain hue to it. Up close, there was a coarseness to Hollister that belied his elegant stage presence. He was a hunter, this boy was. Life's sad wisdom was in his eyes, resting on haunches and ready to spring.

The door opened and Marty Sievers poked his head in, glanced around as if looking for someone, then gave Nudger and Hollister a smile and a little half-salute and withdrew. Nudger wondered if Sievers had been listening outside and perhaps been forced by someone's presence to open the door and look in to avoid the appearance of eavesdropping.

"How well do you know Ineida Mann?" Nudger asked.

"Well enough to know you've been bothering her," Hollister replied, with the bored yet wary expression of an animal sunning itself on a rock. "We don't know what your angle is, but I suggest you stop pestering Ineida." He seemed almost lulled by his own smug confidence. "Don't bother trying to get any information out of me, either."

"No angle," Nudger said. "I'm interested in jazz."

"Among other things."

"Sure; like most people, I have more than one interest."

"Not like me, though," Hollister said. "My only interest is my music. You might call it my consuming passion."

"What about Miss Mann?"

"I told you that's none of your business. You don't listen worth a damn." Hollister stood up, neatly but ineffectively snubbed out the cigarette he'd been smoking, and seemed to relish leaving it to smolder to death slowly in the ashtray. "I've got a number coming up in a few minutes." He tucked in his Fat Jack's T-shirt and looked severe, squaring his shoulders. Obviously this was threat time. "I don't particularly want to see you anymore, Nudger. Whoever, whatever you are, it doesn't mean burned grits to me as long as you leave Ineida alone."

"You shouldn't joke about grits south of the Mason-Dixon line."

"You're the only one taking it as a joke," Hollister said, moving toward the door.

"Before you leave," Nudger said, "can I have your autograph?"

Incredibly, far from being insulted by this sarcasm, Hollister scrawled his signature on a nearby folded newspaper and tossed it to Nudger, as if it were of great value and might serve as a bribe to keep Nudger away from Ineida. Nudger took that as a measure of the man's artistic ego, and despite himself he was impressed. All the ingredients of greatness resided in Willy Hollister, along with something else.

Nudger stuck the folded newspaper in his sportcoat pocket and walked back out into the club. He peered through the throng of jazz lovers and saw Fat Jack at the bar. The crowd was lively tonight, lots of talk and laughter, and there seemed to be a larger than usual percentage of females. Maybe it was ladies' night.

Marty Sievers was leaning with his back against a wall

near the stage, his gaze sliding back and forth over the crowd.

Sidling around a knot of revelers, Nudger made his way across the dim room toward the leviathan form of Fat Jack, so they could talk before Hollister's next set. Just then he spotted Ineida across the room. She was wearing a sequined green blouse that set off her dark hair and eyes and gave her a faintly Gypsy air. Nudger regretted that she couldn't sing as good as she looked. She glanced at him sloe-eyed, recognized him, and quickly turned away to listen to a graying, bearded man who was one of the party at her table. He seemed pleased and surprised by her sudden interest; he removed a curve-stemmed pipe from his mouth, and began to gesture knowingly with it as pipe smokers habitually do. Nudger wondered if his own IQ would rise if he took up smoking a pipe.

"Hey, Nudger," Fat Jack said, when Nudger had reached the bar, "you sure you know what you're doing, old sleuth? You ain't exactly pussyfooting. Ineida asked me about you, said you'd bothered her at home. Hollister asked me who you were. The precinct captain asked me the same question. I feel like I'm on 'The Joker's Wild' and you're my category."

Nudger's stomach tightened. "A New Orleans police captain?"

Fat Jack nodded. "You betcha. Captain Raoul Livingston." He smiled broad and bold and took a sip of absinthe. "You make ripples big enough to swamp boats."

"Do you know anything about this Livingston?"

"Sure," Fat Jack said. "In my business, I'd better know about him. He acts like he's the one that wrote the law and can damn well change it if he wants to as he goes along."

"Tough cop?"

"They say so."

"Who're 'they'?"

"The ones that've had dealings with Livingston. I guess you'll be one of them as soon as he catches up with you."

Nudger thought it was time to change the direction of the conversation. He motioned with his head. "Who's the gray-haired guy with Ineida? The one with the pipe."

"That's Max Reckoner." Fat Jack absently swirled his absinthe around in his glass. "He's a big jazz buff and antique dealer; got himself a string of shops that sell the real stuff as well as reproductions. You might say he's interested in Ineida, and not in a fatherly fashion."

"What does she think of him?" Nudger asked.

"She tolerates him while fending him off nicely without hurting his feelings."

"Does he know who she really is?"

"If he does, he's not saying. He wouldn't. Max is a good enough guy; he's just got glands younger than he is and a wife that understands him too well. That's her near the end of the table, the tall brunette."

"How about Marty Sievers? Does he know Ineida's true identity?"

"Marty? Naw, he's got no idea. Hey, you want a drink?"

"No, thanks."

"Sandwich or something from the kitchen?"

"Nope."

"What then, old sleuth?"

"What I'd like to do now," Nudger said, "is take a short trip."

"Lots of folks would like for you to do that."

"I need to go to Cleveland, Kansas City, St. Louis, and Chicago," Nudger said, sounding like a public-address announcer at a train station. "I'll spend maybe a few hours, maybe a couple of days at the most in each city. I've got to find out some background on Willy Hollister if I'm going to help you. Are you willing to pick up the tab?"

"I don't suppose you could get this information with long-distance phone calls?"

"Not and get it right."

"When do you plan on leaving?"

"Tonight, as soon as I can."

Fat Jack nodded. He produced a checkbook with an alligator cover, scribbled deftly in it, and tore out a check and handed it to Nudger. Nudger squinted at it but couldn't make out the amount in the faint light.

"Hey, if you need more, let me know," Fat Jack said. His smile was luminous in the dimness. "Make it a fast trip, Nudger. I'd like to wind this thing up as soon as possible."

"Speaking of winding up," Nudger said, "do you know anything about a couple of muscular robots? One has a scar across his right eyebrow and a face like an ex-pug's. His partner has a dark mustache, sniper's eyes, and is named Frick. Possibly the other is Frack. They both talk with thick Cajun accents."

Fat Jack raised his eyebrows. Fear caused him to reel out a flag-sized white handkerchief and wipe his forehead. "That'd be Rocko Boudreau and Dwayne Frick," he said, with soft, terror-inspired awe. "They work for David Collins."

"I figured they might. They warned me to stay away from Ineida." Nudger felt his intestines twist into Boy Scout advanced knots. He got out his antacid tablets and placed two on his tongue. "They suggested that if I didn't take their advice, I might take up postmortem residence in the swamp." As he recalled his conversation with Frick and Frack, Nudger again felt a dark near-panic well up in him. Maybe it was because he was pressed in at the bar with the huge and terrified Fat Jack McGee; maybe fear actually was contagious. He offered Fat Jack an antacid tablet. The big man accepted, chewed the tablet furiously, and washed it down with absinthe. Nudger didn't think it would do him much good.

"I'm sure their job is to look after Ineida without her knowing it," Nudger said. "Incidentally, they seem to approve of her seeing Willy Hollister."

"That won't help me for diddly shit if anything happens to Ineida that's in any way connected to the club," Fat Jack said. "It'll be Swamp City for the friendly fat man."

From what he'd heard about David Collins, Nudger thought Fat Jack might not be exaggerating. Frick and Frack were in Collins' employ for more than just keeping things dusted and running out for canapés.

Nudger pushed away from the bar. He was tired and uncomfortable. His stomach was trying to digest itself. "I'd better make airline reservations and pack," he said. "I'll be back as soon as I can."

Fat Jack mumbled something unintelligible and nodded, lost in his own dark apprehensions, a ponderous man grappling with ponderous problems. One of his inflated hands floated up in the dimness in a pale parting gesture.

As Nudger was about to walk away, Willy Hollister launched into his first number.

Nudger hung around and listened. Fat Jack understood.

VII

Where have you been?" Claudia Bettencourt asked Nudger.

"Cleveland, Kansas City, Chicago." "Sounds like three years' worth of Shriners' conventions."

"I've also been to New Orleans," Nudger said, wincing at the morning light blasting through the blinds into Claudia's bedroom. "That's where my new case is. I tried to phone you before I left, but you weren't home."

Claudia slipped into her blue robe and shook her head with brief violence. Her hair was still damp from the shower, and drops of water marked the robe. It was a new robe, with silk at the sleeves and hem, and came down only about halfway to her knees. It made her legs look great. "You might have phoned before you came by last night."

"At midnight when I got into town? Miss Manners would have something disapproving to say about that."

Claudia smiled. "So you just used your key to let yourself in and climbed into bed with me. Perfect etiquette."

"Seemed like a good idea at the time. Does now."

She said something to him, but at the same time she switched on her blow-drier and Nudger couldn't understand her. He lay back in the bed and watched her shake her long dark hair again as she played the hot stream of air over it. She'd let it grow the past six months; he liked it long. She had fleshed out during the past half year, too, and he liked that. She was still slim, and her slender features were still dominated by a nose that was too long but somehow lent her a noble look. Her face was less gaunt now, her hipbones less prominent in bed; she seemed healthier, which immensely pleased Nudger.

Claudia switched off the drier and began brushing her hair in front of her dresser mirror, slouching down slightly with a dancer's grace to fix her entire reflection in the glass. She was using an odd-looking brush with blunted, widely spaced bristles, the sort of thing that sold for something-ninety-nine via TV mail-order commercials.

"How's work?" Nudger asked, meshing his fingers behind his head on the pillow.

"It's fine." She caught his gaze in the mirror and smiled ever so slightly as their eyes locked. Nudger had helped to get her the position as teacher in a private girls' high school in St. Louis County. Apparently she'd taken to her return to teaching after her stint as a waitress, and everything Nudger heard indicated that Stowe School had taken to her. "I've got to go in to work later today," she said.

"It's Saturday."

"I know. I have to grade some tests."

"You could have brought them home."

"I'd rather work at the school." The brush made surprisingly loud, abrupt swishing sounds as she forced it through her still-damp hair. It was a sound Nudger didn't care for. "What kind of case are you working on in New Orleans?" she asked.

"Something to do with a jazz pianist." Nudger didn't elaborate. She knew he didn't like to discuss his cases except when he was ready, if at all, and she wouldn't push. Occasionally there were things about his work that Claudia preferred not knowing.

"Sounds interesting" was all she said. *Shhhhk!* went the brush.

"The layovers in the other cities were to gather background information."

Claudia nodded, not looking at him. *Shhhhk!*

"Stop that, will you?"

"Stop what?" she asked, putting down the brush.

"Never mind." Nudger swung out of bed and padded barefoot toward the bathroom to shower. The hardwood floor was pleasantly cool to walk on.

"One egg or two?" she asked, as he passed her on the way to the door.

"I thought we'd have breakfast out."

"I don't mind cooking," she said. "I still enjoy playing with the kitchen." She had only been in the south St. Louis apartment on Wilmington a little over a month. Considering the roach palace she'd occupied downtown, Nudger could understand why she liked her new kitchen.

"Two eggs," he said, and stepped over his wadded white J. C. Penney underwear where he'd tossed it last night in the throes of passion. Fortunately he kept a complete change of clothes at Claudia's.

In the spacious old tiled bathroom, he stood beneath the stinging needles of a hot shower and thought about Claudia. Her world had improved vastly since her suicide attempt only nine months ago. She had her job, the new apartment, a self-respect she'd thought was lost forever. And Nudger liked to think he was an incentive for her to keep on living. It was nice to be needed.

He began to lather his travel-tired body. The soap was perfumed and had the consistency of whipped cream, but it would have to do.

Nudger felt better after showering and dressing. By the time he walked into the kitchen, the fresh-perked coffee scent had honed his appetite. He sat down across the table from Claudia. She had his sunny-side-up eggs ready, along with black coffee, buttered toast, and three slices of bacon. Working woman though she was, Claudia liked to cook and was good at it. Nudger and his stomach appreciated this touch of domesticity in his otherwise unruly life.

"Are you going to see Nora and Joan today?" he asked, sprinkling too much salt on his eggs. Nora and Joan were Claudia's thirteen- and eleven-year-old daughters by her unfortunate marriage. The girls lived with their father, Ralph Ferris, in north St. Louis County.

Claudia took a sip of coffee. "No, Ralph is taking them out of town this weekend. Or says he is. The bastard."

Nudger smiled. *Bastard.* It was good to hear her refer to Ralph that way. Emotion out in the open. "In touch with her feelings," was the jargon. Her psychiatrist, Dr. Oliver, would like that. Besides, Ralph was undeniably a bastard.

"I'll spend most of the day reading my English Two class's essays on Shelley," she said.

"Winters or Berman?"

"What are you going to do today?" Claudia asked. She had learned to tune out his nonsense. She doused ketchup over her eggs. Nudger didn't understand how she could eat them that way. Or even look at them directly.

"I'm going to see an old friend," he said. "He's not nearly as literate as your English Two class; he communicates best through a saxophone. But he does it oh so eloquently."

Claudia looked up from her colorfully abused eggs and frowned at him. For a moment he thought she was going to ask him to elaborate, but she didn't. She picked up her fork instead.

"Eat your breakfast," she said simply.

Nudger did. Then he kissed her good-bye and left, wiping his mouth with the back of his hand. Ketchup.

Billy Weep lived in a second-floor apartment on Hodimont Avenue on the city's north side. That wasn't his real name, Billy Weep. Nudger had been told what it was one time long ago, but he'd forgotten it. He figured it didn't matter. Not to him, probably not to Billy.

Nudger trudged up narrow dim stairs that reeked of stale urine, then knocked on the first door on his right.

He stood for a few minutes, then knocked again. Harder. There was a faint noise from inside that Nudger chose to interpret as an invitation to enter. He tried the knob, found the door unlocked, and pushed it open.

The one-room apartment smelled worse than the stairwell, but different. It had about it that unmistakable acrid odor of perspiration and futility that suggested illness. Nudger stopped and stood still, as if he'd been hit, when the heat and stench of the place reached him.

The curtains on the single window were pulled almost closed. Squinting in the dim light, Nudger saw an unmoving figure seated in a small chair alongside the window. For a moment he thought he'd walked in on a corpse, then the figure jerked slightly and turned a lean, silhouetted head to stare at him.

"Billy?" Nudger said.

"You askin' or tellin'?" came a high-pitched, weary voice from the chair. It was a voice that had been made monotonal by pain.

"It's Nudger, Billy. I used to come hear you play at Rush's a few years back. We had some drinks together. I did some work for you once."

"Few years back, shit," Billy Weep said. "That's been eight years ago I had you follow Laverne."

Nudger thought about it. Maybe it had been that long since Billy had hired him to get the evidence he'd needed to divorce the wife he didn't trust. It had been one of Nudger's easier tasks, until a strung-out trumpet player had leapt out of Laverne Weep's bed and tried to strangle him. Laverne had joined the struggle, wielding a high-heeled shoe like a club. Nudger had barely gotten out of there alive and still had scars from that night.

"Where'd you get my address?" Billy asked.

"The Musicians' Association down on Fifty-ninth Street. I had to talk it out of them; don't you want to be found?"

"Not these days."

"Why not?"

"These days ain't the old days." A thin, almost twiglike arm rose against the faint light and pulled open the curtains. "Arther-itis," Billy said, holding up his hands in the sunlight so Nudger could see them clearly. The long, slender fingers that had once danced on Billy's alto sax keys were unbelievably contorted. Billy flexed the pathetic fingers to show Nudger that they wouldn't meet the palms of his hands. "Arther-itis is a bitch, Nudger."

Nudger tried to keep the pity from pulling at his face. It wasn't only Billy's hands that looked bad. The man himself couldn't weigh more than ninety pounds, most of that flesh-draped, protruding bone. Billy Weep, who had done magic on the sax, didn't look now as if he had the strength even to stand up with the heavy instrument. Arthritis is a bitch, all right, Nudger thought. Time is a bitch. Eventually, for all of us.

He looked around at the steamy, disheveled apartment. He didn't see what he'd expected, but then the place was still dim, even with the opened curtains. "You been drinking, Billy?"

"No," Billy said, "not drink."

Nudger walked over to stand nearer to the old, old man of fifty-two. "I'll speak straight with you," he said.

"You always did, Nudger."

"You look like death not even warmed over. You killing yourself on something, Billy?"

"Maybe." Narrow, bony shoulders lifted in a slight shrug. Billy turned to stare out the window and the slanted morning light fell across his harshly lined thin face. They were not good lines, not laugh lines. "It don't make me no difference, Nudger. Shouldn't make you none."

Which was Billy's way of suggesting that Nudger mind his own business. Which was what Nudger did.

"Ever hear of a piano player named Willy Hollister?" he asked. He looked past Billy out the window. Nice view. A boarded-up store next to an auto body shop that seemed to do most of its work outdoors. Three cars were up on blocks near the sidewalk, missing various fenders, hoods, and wheels.

"I heard of him," Billy said.

A lithe young black man lowered himself onto a wheeled creeper and got himself comfortable on his back, then kicked his way under a car. Nudger waited. Billy's mind was probably in the same sad shape as his hands; he might need time to think.

"White boy, wasn't he? Blond?"

"Sounds like him, Billy."

"He was a helluva player, that boy," Billy said, still staring out the window, not seeming at all interested in what was out there. Not seeming interested in anything. The world was a rundown record.

"When did you last see him, Billy?"

"Oh, about four years or so ago. He did a gig at Rush's, then he moved on someplace."

"Kansas City?"

"Mighta been." Billy slowly shook his head. "Truth is, I disremember, Nudger. But I do recall how that boy played and sang. We used to jam in at Rush's and listen to him. He was a draw in them days, him and Jack Collinsworth and Fat Jack McGee. They all played at Rush's."

Nudger wasn't really surprised. "You know Fat Jack McGee?"

Billy almost smiled. "Sure, ever'body know the fat man. Jazz be a small world, Nudger."

"Who were Hollister's friends while he played in St. Louis?" Nudger asked.

"No friends. Hollister kept to himself by himself. Except for that Jacqui."

"Jacqui?"

"Yeah, spelled it with a *q-u-i*, said she was some kinda Indian. No chance, the way she looked."

"Do you remember her last name?"

"James. Jacqui James. Not her real name, I suspect. But then neither is Weep my real name."

"Tell me about her, Billy."

"She was a lady in the old true sense, Nudger. She sang a bit, but not much,'cause she knew she didn't have it musically. What she did have was Hollister."

Nudger sat down in an ancient wing chair with perpetually exploding cotton batting and leaned toward Billy. "Where can I find Jacqui James?"

Billy laughed a weak, airless kind of chuckle that was almost a gurgle. He didn't have much lung left. "Ain't nobody can find Jacqui James. She just up and went one day. Nobody ever found out where."

"What about Hollister?"

"What about him? He was heart-an'-soul wrecked by her leavin' like that, Nudger. You could hear the pain of it in his music when he finally admitted to himself that she was gone for good. He played real blues then. The best blues played in them days was at Rush's, but none better than Willy Hollister's blues."

"Then you think he really loved this Jacqui James."

Billy's wide bloodless lips curled up in the cruel light. "Ain't no doubt he loved her, Nudger."

"Do you think he might have had anything to do with her disappearance?" Nudger asked.

Billy shook his head slowly. "Naw, that boy wouldn't have done nothin' to hurt Jacqui. She just up an' gone one day, Nudger. Jacqui was like that. Pretty girl, red hair and green eyes, heart like a cottonwood seed . . . driftin' here an' away in the easiest wind . . .

Nudger stood up. He had to get out of there, away from the heat and stench. He wished he could get Billy away, but he knew it was useless to try. He wondered what the frail, used-up jazz man was taking that had eaten him up so from the inside.

"Thanks, Billy," Nudger put his hands in his pockets. "You, uh . . . ?"

"I don't need nothin', Nudger. I thank you, but I don't. Never did. I'll continue on that way, if you please."

Nudger smiled down at him. "Okay. And I was going to offer you an air conditioner for that window."

Billy grinned a toothy, yellow grin at him. "Your ass, you was, Nudger. The landlord here don't allow no air conditioners. Anyways, you could never even afford a down payment on your bar tab."

Nudger spread his arms slightly in a brief, helpless gesture. "That hasn't changed, except from time to time." He moved toward the door. The man under the car across the street began banging a hammer in slow rhythm against metal.

"Poverty's a disease, Nudger, an' you only got the sniffles." Billy waved a misshapen dark hand around in an encompassing gesture. "This here's what you got to look forward to if you don't straighten out your act. Let me warn you, this is what happens to everybody's good old days."

"I'll hold that cheerful thought," Nudger said. "Go easy on yourself, Billy. You deserve it."

"Hey," Billy said feebly, when Nudger had opened the door. "You still got that jazz-record collection of yours?

Nudger shook his head no. "I had to sell most of it. I could only save the best."

"You save any of mine?"

"Sure I did, Billy."

The contorted hand yanked the curtains closed again. "That's right," came the thin voice from the darkness, "you did say the best."

The relentless banging of metal on metal was still coming from beneath the wrecked car as Nudger walked down the street to his Volkswagen and drove away. The hammer bounced once after each blow: *BANG-bang! BANG-bang! BANG-bang!* . . . sending up a flat rhythm. The weary, frustrated sound hung over the ghetto like a cold, inhuman heartbeat that Nudger could hear for blocks. A dirge for dead dreams.

He stopped at a hardware store and bought a cheap two-speed box fan and paid extra to have it delivered to Billy Weep's address. It wasn't an air conditioner, but it was all Nudger could afford at the moment and it would help, if Billy took the trouble to switch it on.

Nudger had spent some good hours at Rush's listening to Billy Weep's smooth and plaintive alto sax. It was time he gave something back.

When he left the hardware store he drove east on Olive toward downtown and the Third District police station. On a scrap of paper from the glove compartment, so he wouldn't forget, he scribbled the name Jacqui James.

VIII

I need to know about a Jacqui James," Nudger said to Hammersmith, in Hammersmith's office in the Third District station house. "Spelled with a *q-u-i.* "

Lieutenant Jack Hammersmith leaned his obese self back in his comfortable upholstered desk chair and motioned for Nudger to sit in one of the straight-backed wooden chairs before the desk.

"You been gone for two days, Nudge," Hammersmith said, "then you walk in here without even phoning you're coming, and ask me about somebody I never heard of. You in some kind of a rush?"

"Sort of." Nudger sat down. He knew it wouldn't be for long; Hammersmith's visitors' chairs were torture devices designed to keep conversations short and to the point, so the lieutenant would have plenty of time alone for business and smoking his malodorous greenish cigars without anybody complaining or vomiting.

"I phoned your office, Nudge, and talked to nothing but a machine," Hammersmith said. "I phoned your apartment, Claudia's place, Danny's Donuts, all your haunts." Hammersmith's blue eyes were twinkling; he was enjoying this. "No Nudger. All gone. Frankly I was concerned."

"Maybe you should have notified the police."

Hammersmith smiled, got a cigar out of his shirt pocket, and laid it on the desk in the way a suspicious poker player might lay a revolver on the table before the deal. There would be no nonsense here, or there would be fire and smoke.

"I was in New Orleans," Nudger said.

"Hard-earned vacation?"

"Business. Why were you trying to contact me?"

Hammersmith toyed with the cigar, rolling it back and forth a few rotations each way on the desk. He liked to tease before answering a question. "I thought you ought to know that Hugo Rumbo is out on bail."

Hammersmith was referring to a house-sized person who had made life dangerous for Nudger during his last case. Nudger nodded. "Thanks for letting me know, Jack."

"You worried?"

"I should be but I'm not. I don't think Rumbo is bright enough to hold a grudge."

"Maybe not," Hammersmith said. He stopped rolling the cigar. "So what's a Jacqui James?"

"A female of the disappeared type. She was the girifriend of a jazz musician here in town about four years ago when she dropped from sight."

Hammersmith raised his sleek eyebrows. "Foul play?"

"No, he's a hell of a pianist."

Hammersmith unwrapped the cigar and placed it between even, tobacco-stained teeth. "Each year it's easier for me to understand why you had to quit the department. You're not an organization man, Nudge. There is no hole for a peg shaped like you. I assume you want me to check with Missing Persons to see if they have a file on this woman."

"Exactly."

While he pretended to consider this request, Hammersmith fired up the cigar, puffed and wheezed, and exhaled a tremendous dense cloud of greenish smoke. Then, cigar still in his mouth, he lifted the desk phone receiver and punched out the number for the main switchboard. "Get me Mishing Pershons," he said around the cigar.

Nudger smiled at him. Hammersmith smiled back and blew smoke.

"It'll take a few minutes," Hammersmith said, after hanging up the phone. "If there is an MP file on Jacqui James and it's in the computer, we can get a printout of it here for you to read."

"I appreciate this, Jack."

"And so you should."

Nudger had never doubted that Hammersmith would let him use police-department files. The two men had a mutual trust and interdependence going back over a decade to when they had been partners in a two-man patrol car. Hammersmith knew why Nudger had quit the department. It was nerves, a stomach that never got used to the everyday stress and occasional violence that was a patrol cop's lot. In a shoot-out with a burglar in the dark, Nudger had saved Hammersmith's life, though he might just as easily have killed him with one of his shaky, panicky shots.

The nerves had become worse after that, and the department had taken Nudger off patrol duty and turned him into Coppy the Clown, a local TV character who taught young children not to be afraid of policemen in our warped society. But a new police chief had decided that a clown wasn't, after all, the most desirable symbol of the department, and Nudger had resigned rather than return to the grinding stress of patrol duty. He'd become, out of necessity born of knowing no other line of work, a private investigator. It enabled him to pay the bills, more or less, in his journey along life's perilous streets. His nervous stomach traveled right along with him.

"What are you working on in New Orleans?" Hammersmith asked.

"I'm investigating an employee," Nudger said vaguely.

"I won't ask why the employer didn't hire a local," Hammersmith said. "Maybe an investigator with a Louisiana PI license."

"My client wanted only me. I came highly recommended by Jeanette Boyington."

Hammersmith emitted a foul cloud of greenish smoke and chuckled. "Unpredictable bitch, eh?"

"Agreed," Nudger said. "Actually, I'm trying to find out about a man named Hollister, a jazz musician who used to be chummy with Jacqui James."

"Why?" Hammersmith asked bluntly.

"He's involved with another woman, a fellow employee who's the daughter of a big-clout guy named Collins."

Hammersmith removed the cigar from his mouth and looked over its glowing tip at Nudger. There was cool alarm in his blue eyes. "David Collins?"

Nudger shifted his weight to his left haunch, uncomfortable in the hard chair. "How do you know Collins?" he asked. His stomach presaged the answer by arranging itself in what felt like a tight coil.

"I know *of* Collins," Hammersmith said, "and that's as close as I care to get. Mostly what I've heard is rumor, but none of it is good rumor. Involvement in a Gulf Coast real estate scam, a series of inflated construction bids and kickbacks when the New Orleans World's Fair was being put together, whispers of a Collins cut in a big South American drug operation that was drop-shipping in southern Florida. Collins is purported to be more of a financier of crime than an actual participant. He keeps himself at least twice-removed and free from prosecution."

"Interesting," Nudger said, "but how does a police lieutenant in St. Louis happen to know all about David Collins in New Orleans?"

"There are people who are connected in every major city," Hammersmith said. "Upper-echelon cops everywhere know who they are, or at least should know, because crime is an interstate business."

Nudger's stomach lurched into fiery contortions, almost doubling him over in his chair. " 'Connected,' you said? 'Business,' you said?"

Hammersmith nodded. "I said." He carefully angled the cigar in the glass ashtray so it wouldn't go out, then squinted through the smoke, trying to gauge the effect of his words on Nudger.

"You mean the Mafia?" Nudger asked.

Hammersmith shrugged. "Who can say for sure? But whatever or whoever runs things in a big way has an umbrella over Collins. Don't try to rain on him, Nudge."

"I'm not," Nudger said. "Well, not exactly. Maybe just a fine mist."

Hammersmith grunted dubiously, picked up his cigar, and resumed his smokestack act, leaving Nudger to his own dire thoughts.

A few minutes later there was a respectful light knock on the door and a pimply-faced young civilian clerk entered the office and placed a yellow file folder on Hammersmith's desk. He withdrew quickly, almost genuflecting, and Hammersmith opened the folder and read for several minutes before speaking again to Nudger. Nudger noticed that his old partner was leaning back from the material on his desk and wondered if Hammersmith had reached the age where he needed glasses.

Still without looking up, Hammersmith scratched a jowly, smooth-shaven cheek and said, "Jacqueline Jamison, a.k.a. Jacqui James, was reported missing January twenty-fourth, four years ago. Female Caucasian, twenty-six years old then, average height and weight, auburn hair and green eyes, no distinguishing marks, last seen wearing a white cotton blouse, blue cotton skirt, blah, blah, blah."

"Who reported her missing?" Nudger asked, trying to envision a cotton blah, blah, blah.

"Says here the apartment manager where she lived, a Miss Irma Gorman, address over on Alabama Avenue. Jacqui James hadn't paid her rent or been seen for a while, so Irma Gorman took legal steps to get her possessions out of the apartment so she could rent it to another tenant."

"What did the investigation turn up?" Nudger asked.

"Ah, here we get to Jacqui James close up and personal. A show-biz type on the fringes. She worked around town as a singer, had no close family, and drug paraphernalia was found in her apartment. Also, she had an arrest record. Two controlled-substance charges and one misdemeanor—shoplifting under a hundred dollars. Suspended sentences, never served time for anything. Minor stuff, Nudge."

"What kind of singer?"

"I never caught her act," Hammersmith said. "I'm no judge of talent anyway. But the report says she sang opera and blues. Humph!"

"Is there a photograph in the file?" Nudger asked.

Hammersmith nodded, turning the open file folder on the desk so Nudger could see inside.

Jacqui James looked young and fresh except for her

eyes, which harbored a subtle sadness. Her black-and-white snapshot was slightly out of focus, and she stared out of the file folder at Nudger through a kind of haze, maybe the sun in the camera lens. There were trees and a small lake in the background. She was an ordinary-looking young woman, with a pretty, oval face. If she wasn't the Ineida Collins type, she was far from the opposite.

"Was she ever reported seen anywhere after the landlady said she was missing?" Nudger asked.

Hammersmith closed the file folder and shook his head. "No, this MP report is the last of Jacqui James in St. Louis as far as the police are concerned. And frankly, Nudge, she's not the sort of MP who's searched for around every corner. She was a known user and worked irregularly as an entertainer. Those people tend to be transient. Night people. It's not unusual for them to disappear with the morning light. Maybe she owed her supplier and couldn't come up with payment. Maybe she met a man. Maybe she just got up one morning with an itch to change the scenery around her." Hammersmith leaned back with his cigar and added to the considerable pollution in the tiny office. "Now, if you don't mind, Nudge, crime of a more recent nature needs tending."

Nudger stood up, finding the haze denser nearer the ceiling. It made his eyes water. He thanked Hammersmith for the information and started toward the door.

"Don't take chances around David Collins," Hammersmith cautioned from behind another billowing green cloud. "You're skating on thin ice over deep water. And your few friends who might pull you out and dry you off are here and not in New Orleans."

Sage advice, Nudger thought, even if offered in the wrong season. He nodded good-bye and left Hammersmith alone in air that only he could breathe.

As he walked across the station house's black-top parking lot, where his battered Volkswagen squatted patiently in a visitors' slot, Nudger thought about the long-gone Jacqui James. Hammersmith was right; she wasn't the sort of woman who would be searched for with any real effort. Not like Ineida Collins, who would be searched for with everything from bloodhounds to spy satellites. Of course, Willy Hollister didn't know that; to him, Ineida Collins was Ineida Mann, and probably didn't seem much different from Jacqui James, who was or had been the kind of independent, unfettered woman that Ineida only pretended to be. Jacqui James had been burned; Ineida Collins was still flitting experimentally around the alluring flame. It was a flame that might have claimed more than one victim. That still burned fiercely.

Nudger got into the sun-heated Volkswagen and drove to Jacqui James' last known address, wondering if he was the only person anywhere who still cared about what might have happened to her.

IX

Jacqui James had lived in a six-family brick apartment building in a bad block of Alabama in south St. Louis. The building's wood trim was blistered and cracked, parched for paint, and chunks of the facade up near the flat roof had crumbled away to leave irregular gaps. The top of the building reminded Nudger of a jaw with teeth missing.

Nudger checked the mailboxes in the littered, graffiti-profaned vestibule and saw that the manager lived in 2-D. He was pleased to see that the name was still Miss I. Gorman. He went up the stairs to the landing and knocked on the door.

Irma Gorman surprised Nudger. He'd expected an older woman. She looked no more than twenty-five, and was plump, blue-eyed, and attractive. The material of her blue blouse gaped, straining at the white buttons down her breast. Her designer jeans were tight everywhere, as if encasing her were a privilege they never wanted to give up.

"Miss Gorman?"

She nodded.

"Are you the Irma Gorman who was manager here four years ago, when Jacqui James was reported missing?"

For a moment the doll-like blue eyes were blank. Then they sharpened with remembrance and maybe wariness. "I'm the one who reported Miss James missing. Has she been found?"

"Not yet. Can I come in and ask you a few questions?"

"You a policeman?"

"Nope, private detective."

"Oh, yeah?" Irma Gorman said, brightening. She was going to tell him . . . and did: "I never met a real private detective."

"Disappointed?" Nudger asked.

She shrugged and stepped back to let him enter.

The decor of her apartment was early Sears with K-Mart accessories. Unlike the vestibule that she managed, it was clean and neatly arranged. There was a kind of homey quality to it that Nudger liked. Through a door he could see stacks of papers, some tagged keys, and a calculator on a Formica table. The trappings of apartment-managing biz.

"Please sit down, Mr.—?"

"Nudger." He sat on a stiff, plaid early American sofa that probably unfolded into a stiff, plaid bed.

"You want anything to drink?"

"No, thanks, just answers." Nudger leaned his head back against the thick roll of upholstery along the top of the sofa.

"Do you want me to tell you about Jacqui James' disappearance?"

"Mostly about Jacqui James herself," Nudger said.

Irma Gorman sat down in a small vinyl chair, putting added strain on her jeans, and compressed her cupid's-bow lips thoughtfully. She was round-faced, sweetly pretty, and in twenty years would be a dumpling of a woman and look

like the sort of good-natured hausfrau who could make terrific strudel. She'd be just right for Germanic south St. Louis.
"Jacqui only lived here about nine months, and she kinda
kept to herself. Oh, she was nice enough and would chat if
she ran into somebody in the hall, but mostly she was quiet.
Not stuck up, but sort of above things. What you might call
classy."

"Did she pay her rent on time?"

"Hardly ever. But that ain't unusual in this neighborhood, Mr. Nubber."

"Nudger. Did any of your other tenants ever complain
about her?"

"Only about her playing her stereo too loud sometimes.
But that ain't unusual in this neighborhood, or in any apartment building these days, either. She was a singer and she'd
sing along with her records. Hard rock and jazz and all that.
Even opera. I don't like any of it, myself."

Nudger smiled. "You look like the Mills Brothers type."

"Who're they?"

"Never mind. When did you notice Jacqui James was
missing?"

"When the rent was three weeks late. I'd been up to her
apartment a dozen times, knocking on her door, but I didn't
get any answer. I phoned, too, thinking she might be watching out her peephole and avoiding me; tenants do that
sometimes. She didn't answer her phone, neither. Finally I
figured maybe she'd moved out on the sly, so I took my
passkey and opened her door to see if the place was still furnished. It was. And I smelled something rotten and looked
into the kitchen and seen her half-eaten dinner there on the
table, only it had to be weeks old. There was roaches all over
it, looking like a regular dark carpet that moved."

Nudger's stomach tilted and zoomed.

"So I figured I better call the police," Irma Gorman continued. "They came out and looked around, asked some questions, but they didn't seem all that interested. I waited another week, then had the owner's lawyer get me some eviction papers and had her furniture moved out so I could rent the apartment to somebody else."

"Where's her furniture?"

"Her boyfriend came and got it. Billy something."

"Not Willy?"

"Oh yeah, Willy."

"Was his last name Hollister?"

"I can't remember his last name, Mr. Nubber."

"Blond, good-looking man? Sort of thin?"

"That's him. He was some kinda musician. Him and some other men came out and loaded Jacqui's furniture into a rented truck and that was the last I seen of any of them. I was surprised to see you here, still interested in what mighta happened to her."

"Why?"

"Because I'm sure something bad happened to Jacqui, and she ain't coming back or gonna be heard from again. I watched Willy and his friends load the truck and seen what they put in. She left all her clothes in her apartment, and her big stereo that I heard cost over a thousand dollars. Nobody runs away and leaves stuff like that."

That was true enough, Nudger thought. And it was the sort of thing he'd come here to learn about.

"That stereo had four speakers and a digital clock and all kinds of gadgets that lit up and went around while it played. My older sister tried to buy it from that Willy guy, but he said no, he wouldn't sell."

"Did he seem confused or upset about Jacqui's disappearance?"

Irma Gorman cocked her head and thought back. "No, I can't say he seemed anything but normal, from what I saw of him. He probably figured like the police did, that Jacqui was the type to just up and leave. Leastways that's what the police said about her. But I don't think anybody'd do that right in the middle of supper and leave most everything they owned behind, not even somebody in show business, do you?"

"I do not," Nudger said. "Did Willy Hollister visit her often?"

"I can't say for sure; I don't spy. It seemed like he was around her place a lot, though, as I recall."

A squawk from the next room made Nudger jump. Then he realized the sound was made by a baby.

"That's okay, Mr. Nubber, it's little Eddie. 'Scuse me." Irma Gorman got up and hurried into the bedroom. The baby started to cry, then was immediately silent.

Irma's name on the mailbox read "Miss," and she wasn't wearing a wedding ring. None of Nudger's business.

When she returned from the bedroom she had her blouse open and was nursing an infant. "This here is my Eddie."

Nudger swallowed self-consciously and stared at the baby tugging on Irma Gorman's brown nipple. "Cute," he said, hoping Irma wouldn't notice his embarrassment. He'd been born at the wrong time and was still laboring under the inhibitions of most men over forty.

He stood up from the sofa. "I appreciate your help, Miss Gorman. Good-bye. And good-bye, er, Eddie."

"No trouble," Irma said, carrying the nursing baby across the room to see Nudger out. "And good luck."

"Good luck?"

"Sure. I hope you find Jacqui."

Nudger left without telling her he wasn't looking for her missing tenant. He and Irma Gorman shared the same opinion, that something bad had happened to Jacqui James and she wouldn't be seen again.

On the drive to Claudia's apartment, Nudger thought about little Eddie. Whatever the circumstances, a kid could do worse for a mother than Irma Gorman.

"How was school today?" Nudger asked Claudia.

She had just entered the apartment and had plopped a blue loose-leaf notebook stuffed with dog-eared papers onto the table by the door. "School was just fine." She smiled at Nudger and walked over and kissed him lightly on the lips, bending down to reach him where he sat on the sofa. She was dressed in a prim-looking gray dress with a red bow at the neck and a red belt cinching the material tight around her slender waist. Red high-heeled shoes showed off her nicely curved, nyloned ankles. A red garter belt would really go great with that outfit, Nudger thought. The kids at Stowe High School had to think Ms. Bettencourt was their sexiest teacher.

Nudger considered grabbing her and pulling her down to sit on his lap, but she moved away too quickly and walked toward the kitchen. She knew him well enough to have become wily.

He looked back toward the local TV news he'd been watching. A polar bear at the zoo was pregnant; very rare.

Claudia returned a few minutes later with a glass of ice water for herself and Budweiser beer in a glass for Nudger. She handed him the glass and sat down beside him on the sofa.

"I'm going back to New Orleans tonight," Nudger said. He saw her body stiffen slightly, though he continued to watch TV. The news was running a feature; a stout little man in a grocer's apron was telling viewers the things they could do with rutabaga.

"Why so soon?"

"Business." He told her about Fat Jack McGee and Ineida Collins/Mann and Willy Hollister.

"Are you beginning to feel protective toward Miss Mann?" Claudia asked.

"As an uncle might."

Claudia took a sip of water and rested a cool, damp hand on Nudger's arm. "You know I appreciate what you've done," she said, "getting me the job at Stowe School—"

"I didn't get the job, you did," he interrupted.

She ignored him. "—making it possible for me to live with the pain after my marriage."

"Dr. Oliver's the guy to thank for that," Nudger said. The psychiatrist was helping her to cope with the guilt that clung to her, guilt laid on by her former husband, Ralph Ferris. Despicable Ralph.

Claudia smiled and aimed her dark eyes at Nudger. They were deeper than usual and clouded with tears. He didn't want her to cry. "Sure," she said "you weren't any help at all."

"You're not really worried about me getting involved with that girl Ineida, are you?" Nudger asked. He was embarrassed by her gratitude and wanted away from the subject of Nudger as savior.

"No."

He wasn't sure if he believed her. Or if he wanted to believe her.

"I know you, Nudger. If she were a bird with a broken wing, I'd worry. But she has wealth; she'll be able to fly."

"If she gets the chance."

Claudia sloshed the water around in her glass. The ice made faint clinking sounds. "Why don't you go back to New Orleans in the morning instead of tonight?"

Nudger knew he shouldn't delay going back; he'd been gone long enough as it was. Maybe long enough to allow Willy Hollister to make whatever move he had planned for Ineida. But he said, "I might be able to do that." On the news, a group of irate Webster Groves residents were complaining vociferously about a county plan to widen an old scenic street and cut down dozens of stately trees. Hammersmith lived out in Webster Groves, but as far as Nudger knew, cared nothing for trees.

"I can fix us dinner here," Claudia said, knowing the way to male hearts over forty, "and we can spend a quiet evening."

"Do you think it's unrealistic for a forty-three-year-old man to be embarrassed in the presence of a woman breast-feeding her infant?" Nudger asked.

Claudia cocked her head to the side and looked at him. "Yes."

"I think so, too. I wonder why I am."

"It's not unusual. And there might be a lot of reasons. Men your age were subject to youths when female organs were associated with the sex act and nothing else. You're part of the mammary generation, Nudger."

"Not Pepsi?"

"That, too."

"Then I'm sexually repressed?"

"Maybe." Claudia grinned. "Or maybe you're just jealous of the infant."

Nudger propped his stockinged feet up on the coffee table, took a sip of Budweiser, and thought about that.

"Jealous," he said at last.

Claudia's grin widened and her fingers inched toward the buttons on her dress. "No need for that," she said, moving closer. Nudger definitely would change that airline reservation.

From the corner of his eye he saw an old black-and-white photograph of a young Billy Weep on the TV screen, hugging his saxophone to him as if it were a woman and smiling whitely and broadly. A pretty blond anchorwoman who recited the news as if she were reading *The Three Bears* to children was telling about how a one-time well-known local jazz musician was found beaten to death in his Hodimont Avenue apartment.

Nudger changed his plans again.

X

As the DC-10 dipped a wing and descended to circle the New Orleans airport, the old man in the seat next to Nudger's, who had kept dozing off and resting his head on Nudger's shoulder, sat up straight and stared past him out the window, entranced by the up-rushing ground lights.

During the flight south, looking out the window at a night salted with wavering bright stars, Nudger had thought about what Hammersmith told him. There was nothing about Billy Weep's death for the law to latch on to. No sign of forced entry, no revealing fingerprints, no blunt instrument that matched the fatal wounds. Nothing but an old black man dead in an old room. Music and memory finally ceased.

Hammersmith thought maybe it was simply a petty robbery. Weep had been a known user, and there had been no money and nothing drugrelated in the apartment. Billy Weep might have been killed for a few grams of cocaine. Every day, people were murdered for less reason than that.

Nudger suddenly felt queasy as the plane dropped steeply for its landing approach. His ears began to pop.

"Fasten your seat belt, young fella," the old man next to him curtly instructed.

Nudger buckled up for safety. He hadn't done enough of that in life.

Early the next morning, Nudger was sitting across from Fat Jack McGee in the club owner's second-floor office. Fat Jack loomed behind his desk like a misplaced mountain. He had on that nifty cream-colored sport jacket, a white shirt, and a blue silk tie with a gold tie bar and a diamond stick pin. Gold cuff links and a gold wristwatch and chain bracelet peeked from beneath his spotless jacket sleeves. Protruding from his jacket pocket was a blue silk handkerchief that matched the tie, folded in a neat triangle. Nudger had never been able to fold a pocket handkerchief that way; he had some of the fake ones folded by the manufacturer and stapled on little sheets of cardboard, but he never wore them. He sat watching Fat Jack talk on the desk phone and wondered how the big man could wear all that stone and metal and not seem overdressed. It had to be his sheer bulk.

"Hey, yeah," Fat Jack said into the phone. He gave his flesh-upholstered wide grin and winked at Nudger with a glittering piggish eye. "Hey, lemme get back to you later, okay?" He waited a few minutes, then hung up. "Business that'll keep," he explained to Nudger. He placed his elbows on the desk and laced his sausage-sized fingers. Gold glinted. "You got traveling out of your system, old sleuth?"

"For now," Nudger said. "You remember Billy Weep?"

Fat Jack nodded. "Vaguely. Sax man, ain't he?"

"Dead man," Nudger said. "Somebody beat him to death yesterday in his apartment in St. Louis."

Fat Jack looked concerned. "What was it? Argument, robbery, what?"

"It was probably what," Nudger said. "I'd just been to see him that morning."

"Well, now!" Fat Jack said, frowning with meaty brows. "You think there's some connection?"

"I don't know," Nudger said.

Fat Jack shook his broad head. "Something else to worry about, as if I ain't got enough problems. What else did you find out in your travels, other than that Billy Weep died?"

"I went to musicians' unions, jazz people, clubs where Willy Hollister had played, in four cities."

"Were all those miles and conversations necessary?"

"As it turns out, yes," Nudger said. "I picked up a pattern, sometimes strong, sometimes subtle, but always there, like in a forties Ellington piece."

"So tell me about it," Fat Jack said. "I'm an Ellington fan."

"All the people I talked with, all the old reviews I read, everything pieced together gave me a kind of condensed journal of Willy Hollister's ascending career. He always started strong, but his musical life was checkered with flat spots, lapses, times when there was something missing from his music: the sense of soul and pain that makes a blues man great. During those times, Hollister was just an ordinary performer."

Fat Jack appeared worried, tucked his chin back into folds of flesh, and said, "That explains why he's falling off here."

"But the man is still making great music," Nudger said.

"He's slipping from great to good," Fat Jack said. "Good jazz artists in New Orleans I can hire by the barrelful."

"There's something else about Willy Hollister," Nudger said. "Something that nobody picked up on because it spanned a lot of years and four cities."

Fat Jack looked interested.

"Hollister had a steady girlfriend in each of these cities," Nudger told him. "All four women disappeared."

Fat Jack drew back in his chair. "Whaddya mean, 'disappeared'? Like 'poof'?"

"Almost like 'poof.' One day they were there, the next day gone. They were women whose disappearances wouldn't be taken all that seriously by all that many people," Nudger said. "Usually they were performers, or hangers-on at the jazz scene. They were the sort whose jobs or personalities sometimes prompted them to leave town without a lot of prior notice."

"Weren't the police notified of their disappearances?"

"Two of the women were rumored to have left town on their own, and their sudden disappearances weren't reported to Missing Persons. The first woman, in Cleveland, and the third one, in St. Louis, abruptly dropped out of sight, were reported, and are still in the Missing Persons files."

"Whoo, boy!" Fat Jack said. He began to sweat. He pulled his white flag-sized handkerchief from an inside pocket of his neat jacket and mopped his brow, just like Satchmo but without the grin and magic trumpet.

"Sorry," Nudger said. "I didn't mean to make you uncomfortable."

"Hey, you're doing your job, is all," Fat Jack assured him in a wheezy, quavering voice. "But that's bad information to lay on me, Nudger. Bad, bad, bad. I take it you think Hollister had a lot to do with the disappearances of these women."

Nudger shrugged. He knew better than to snatch at the obvious. "Maybe the women themselves, and not Hollister, had everything to do with why they're gone. We can't discount the fact that they were all the sort who traveled light and often." Nudger gave Fat Jack the women's names. The only one he recognized was Jacqui James, but he'd only met her a few times and didn't know she'd disappeared.

Fat Jack bowed his head and looked melancholy, almost ready to sob.

"Maybe the women actually left town of their own accord," Nudger said. "Maybe for some reason they felt they had to get away from Hollister."

"I wish Ineida would want to get away from the bastard," Fat Jack muttered. Then he realized what he'd said. "But Jeez, not like that. Her old man'd boil me down for axle grease if she just disappeared from here. But then she's not cut from the same bolt as those other girls; she's not what she's trying to be and is strictly local."

"The one thing she and those other women have in common is Willy Hollister."

"Ain't no getting away from that," Fat Jack said. He leaned back. Nudger heard the desk chair creak in weary protest. Nudger, who had been hired to solve a problem, had so far only brought to light the seriousness of that problem. Fat Jack was still between a rock and a hard place, and the rock had become larger, the hard place harder. The big man didn't have to ask "What now?" It was written in capital letters on his face.

"We could tell Ineida about Hollister's missing women," Nudger said. When in doubt, say something.

"She wouldn't listen, Nudger. Wouldn't believe anything bad about Hollister if she did listen. Love leads people into trouble that way."

Nudger figured Fat Jack was right. He should know about such things; that was what the blues were about.

"You could fire Willy Hollister," Nudger said.

Fat Jack shook his head. "Ineida would follow him, and maybe get mad at me and sic her dad on the club."

"And Hollister is still packing customers into the club every night."

"That, too," Fat Jack admitted. Even the loosest businessman could see the profit in Willy Hollister's genius. "For now," he said, "I guess we'll let things slide while you continue to watch Hollister and Ineida." He dabbed at his forehead again with the wadded handkerchief. "It'd be my big finale for sure if anything happened to that girl. Her dad would see to that."

"Hollister doesn't know who I am," Nudger said, "but he knows who I'm not and he's worried. My presence might keep him aboveboard for a while."

"Any amount of time looks pretty valuable to me right now," Fat Jack said.

"Meanwhile," Nudger told him, "I'll keep probing for more information. Maybe I'll come up with something that will cause Ineida to have a change of heart about Hollister."

"Fine, as long as a change of scenery isn't involved. I can't afford to have her wind up like those other women, Nudger."

Or like Billy Weep, Nudger thought, as he stood up from his chair. "I'll phone you if I have any more good news," he said.

Fat Jack mumbled something unintelligible and nodded, lost in his vast interior gloom. Things weren't turning out at all the way he'd hoped, and in the past several prosperous years he'd become unused to disappointment. He didn't look up as Nudger walked from the stifling office.

Nudger had his own apprehensions. He had the feeling he'd delved far enough into this matter to have stirred up waters that wouldn't calm easily. What Hammersmith had told him about David Collins' underworld status had caused Nudger's stomach to issue an uncommonly strong warning. His stomach was seldom wrong; it was growling now, something that sounded like "Get ooout!"

He knew that his future, like Fat Jack's, depended almost exclusively on Ineida Collins' wellbeing. He sure hoped that girl didn't do anything foolish.

If Fat Jack wound up playing his clarinet for nickles on some skid-row street corner, Nudger would probably be the one passing the hat.

That's if they were both lucky.

XI

When Nudger got back to his hotel, he was surprised to open the door to his room and see a man sitting in a chair by the window. It was the big blue armchair that belonged near the door. The man had dragged it over to where he could sit comfortably and have a view.

As Nudger entered, the man turned as if resenting the interruption, as if it were his room and Nudger the interloper. He stood up and smoothed his light-tan suit coat. He was a smallish man with a triangular face and very bushy red hair that grew in a sharp widow's peak. His eyes were dark and intense. He resembled a fox more than anyone Nudger had ever seen. With a quick and graceful motion he reached a paw into a pocket for a wallet-size leather folder. He flipped the folder open to reveal a badge. Not an ordinary patrolman's badge, but an officer's fancy three-color one.

"Captain Livingston, I presume," Nudger said. He shut the door and came the rest of the way into the room.

The redheaded man nodded and replaced the badge in

his pocket. "I'm Raoul Livingston," he confirmed. "I think we should talk, Nudger." He shoved the armchair around to face the room instead of the window and sat back down comfortably, as familiar as old shoes.

Nudger pulled out the small wooden desk chair and also sat, facing Livingston. "Are you here on official business, Captain Livingston?"

Livingston smiled. He had tiny sharp teeth behind thin lips that folded back peculiarly when he grinned. "You know how it is, Nudger, a cop is always a cop."

"Sure. And that's the way it is when we go private. A confidential investigator is always that, no matter where he is or who he's talking to."

"Which is kinda why I'm here," Livingston said, tapping a light tattoo on the chair arm with his forefinger. "It might be better if you were someplace else, someplace other than New Orleans."

Nudger was incredulous. His nervous stomach believed what he'd just heard, but his brain didn't. "You're actually telling me to get out of town?"

Livingston gave a snippy kind of laugh, but there was no glint of amusement in his sharp eyes. "I'm not authorized to *tell* anyone to get out of town, Nudger. I'm not the sheriff and this isn't Dodge City."

"I'm glad you realize that," Nudger told him, "because I can't leave yet. I've got business here."

"I know about your business."

"Did David Collins send you?"

Livingston had a good face for police work; there was only the slightest change of expression in his eyes while his features remained set. "We can let that question go by," he said, "and I'll take my turn. Why did Fat Jack McGee hire you?"

"Have you asked him?"

"No."

"He'd rather I kept his reasons confidential," Nudger said. "I'm required to honor the wishes of my client. It's a professional obligation."

"You don't have a Louisiana PI license," Livingston pointed out.

Nudger smiled. "I know. Nothing to be revoked."

Livingston gave him a nasty little smirk, a man faintly annoyed but a long way from losing his temper. "There are consequences a lot more serious than having your investigator's license pulled, Nudger. Mr. Collins would prefer that you stay away from Ineida Mann."

"You mean Ineida Collins."

"I mean what I say."

"David Collins already had someone deliver that brief but succinct message to me."

"It's not a message from anyone but me this time," Livingston said. "I'm telling you this because I'm concerned about your safety while you're within my jurisdiction. It's part of my job."

Nudger kept a straight face, stood up, and walked to the door and opened it. He said, "I appreciate your concern, Captain. Right now, I've got things to do."

Livingston smiled with his mean little mouth. He didn't seem rattled by Nudger's impolite invitation to leave; he'd said what needed saying. He got up out of the armchair and adjusted his suit, smoothing the wrinkles from his pants and pulling the jacket straight with little jerks of the lapels. Nudger noticed that the suit hung on him just so and had to be tailored and expensive. No cop's salary wardrobe for Livingston.

As he walked past Nudger, Livingston paused and said,

"It'd behoove you to learn to discern friend from enemy, Nudger."

"You don't often hear the word 'behoove' anymore," Nudger told him.

" 'Discern,' either," Livingston said. He went out and trod lightly down the hall toward the elevators, not looking back.

Nudger shut and locked the door. Then he went over to the bed, removed his shoes, and stretched out on his back on the mattress. He lay with his right hand behind his head, his left resting lightly on his stomach, which was not too steady. He sucked on an antacid tablet and studied the faint water stains on the ceiling in the corner directly above him. They were old but still damp, covered with a thin green film of mold. Looking at them reminded Nudger of the bayou.

It'd behoove you to learn to discern friend from enemy, Nudger.

He had to admit that Livingston had left him with solid parting advice.

And an added measure of worry.

XII

The next morning Nudger drove the same cramped red subcompact, the matchbox the rental agency seemed to hold in reserve just for him, over to Magazine Street. It wasn't the best part of town, hadn't been for years. He found a parking place halfway down a block of tile-roofed, two-story buildings, each with intricately turned iron railings and long, second-floor balconies that looked too rickety to support much weight. There were a lot of potted plants on the balconies, and some outdoor furniture. Small magnolia trees grew from large, round concrete planters placed every fifty feet or so at the curb. Recent renovation and fresh paint tried hard, but couldn't quite mask the fact that not long ago this had been a run-down neighborhood. That, and the liberal sprinkling of antique shops and small restaurants lining each side of the street, indicated that gentrification was underway here, the process by which a seedy neighborhood suddenly acquires character rather than undesirability, becomes trendy, and, eventually, outrageously expensive.

Nudger guessed that right now this block of Magazine Street was peopled by the mix of old, poorer residents afraid of change, and the new, young professional types, marking the area as trendy but not yet prohibitively overpriced. The longtime residents might still outnumber the newcomers. The rest of the Indians had to be run out before the home-steaders would move here in large numbers.

He unfolded from the subcompact, stood on the side-walk, and stretched the kinks from his spine. He hated little cars. Well, maybe not his comfortably well-worn Volkswa-gen Beetle back in St. Louis, which at least had head room. He had bumped his head twice crossing railroad tracks in this little torture device on wheels.

From the sagging balcony above, a gray, tiger-striped cat observed him with calm disdain. Nudger clucked his tongue at the cat, which caused the animal to blink twice slowly. Nudger wished he had the cat's composure and han-dle on life.

He decided to leave his sportjacket in the car, and walked down the sidewalk while rolling up the sleeves of his white shirt. It was more muggy than hot this morning, but he figured that by noon the heat would catch up with the humidity and turn the city into the sauna of the South.

He stopped beneath a tall yellow sign that proclaimed the shop beneath it to be GOLDEN OLDENS. Nudger had gath-ered from the New Orleans phone directory that this shop was the flagship of the four Golden Oldens antique shops, and the logical place to find Max Reckoner. As with Jud-man, he'd decided against phoning for an appointment; it was seldom enlightening to interview people who'd had a chance to prepare for the conversation.

Nudger pushed open a grained oak door that boasted a leaded glass window and entered the shop.

He was in a large, pleasantly cool room with a glossy bare wood floor. An air conditioner was humming steadily somewhere nearby, and from the high, white ceiling hung four fans with wide, slowly rotating wicker blades, surely moving too lazily to stir the air. The antiques in the place ran heavily to burled walnut, inlaid marble, cut glass, and gleaming Victorian furniture that looked as if just yesterday it had sprung from the gnarled hands of loving craftsmen. Not the kind of antique shop you'd duck into on impulse with ten dollars to shore up your beer-can collection.

Nudger stood enjoying the scent of lemon oil and old wood, while a huge porcelain Chinese dragon with its tongue lolling out leered at him.

A small man with dainty, effeminate features and immaculately styled short blond hair walked around a ten-foot-tall secretary-desk and smiled at Nudger. Apparently the door touched off some sort of signal when a customer entered the shop.

"Yes, sir?" the clerk said. He was wearing a well-cut beige suit with a vest, and incredibly fancy yellow moccasins with white rawhide tassels. There were moccasins and then there were moccasins. If these were made by real Indians, they were rich Indians. This is an expensive place, said his clothes and his bearing.

"Is Max Reckoner in?" Nudger asked, absently resting a hand on the glistening green head of the Chinese dragon. The clerk's large blue eyes flicked reproachfully to the offending hand and Nudger removed it and stuffed it into his pocket as if to punish it.

"I believe he's in his office," the clerk said. His delicate face was stiff and appeared oddly waxy. He wasn't a man who smiled more than a few times a year. "Who shall I say wants him? And what's your business with Mr. Reckoner?"

"My name is Nudger. I'm a private detective. So naturally I'd like to talk to Mr. Reckoner about a private matter."

"Naturally," the clerk said equably, too quick on his tasseled moccasins to be thrown. "Please wait here." He pivoted like a dancer on his left toe and sashayed down a row of looming, curvaceous furniture, then rounded a corner and was gone. Right back into the nineteenth century. Nudger heard a door open and close down the corridor of time. Or maybe it was the door to Reckoner's office, right here in this century.

He stood quietly waiting, studying a collection of Civil War swords mounted on a wall. The South would never rise again if it had to rearm at these prices. The seconds passed, maybe four score and seven. He got tired of swords and watched the rich and poor and blacks and whites and tourists and young urban pioneers walk back and forth on the street beyond the hanging plants in the Golden Oldens' narrow, yellow-tinted shop windows. There sure were a lot of plants in this neighborhood.

"This way, Mr. Nudger," the clerk said behind him.

Nudger jumped, his attention yanked back inside the shop.

He followed the young clerk down the aisle he'd seen him go down previously, flanked by dark old desks, bookcases, wardrobes, and fancy breakfronts. Everything in the shop other than Nudger and the clerk seemed to have claw feet, and Nudger couldn't be sure about the clerk.

The clerk opened a red-lacquered door and ushered Nudger into a spacious, red-carpeted office dominated by a massive Queen Anne desk. Three of the walls were paneled in rich dark walnut; on a fourth wall were a bank of black file cabinets and a table supporting an IBM personal computer. Max Reasoner sat behind the desk, almost dwarfed by it, though he was a rangy six-footer. His beard looked as if it had just been trimmed, and it matched perfectly the gray of his elegant sport jacket. The curve-stemmed pipe lay propped in an antique glass-and-iron ashtray on the desk. Reckoner stood up smoothly, a middleaged guy in good shape, maybe a jogger, and extended his hand toward Nudger.

As they shook hands, Reckoner said off to the side, "Thank you, Norman," and the clerk left the office on little cat feet and closed the door behind him.

"I believe I saw you at Fat Jack's," Reckoner said amiably. He motioned for Nudger to sit down in one of the deep, leather-upholstered chairs before the desk.

Nudger sat, watching Reckoner lower himself easily into his big desk chair. It was modern, yet somehow looked as if it belonged behind the antique desk. "I guess we're both jazz fans," Nudger said.

Reckoner picked up the curve-stemmed pipe, toyed with it, then placed it back in the ashtray. There was self-assurance even in that gesture. He was quite the sophisticate, but he wore it well; it seemed as natural to him as if he'd been born and raised in a big manor house in antebellum Louisiana. His accent, strangely enough, sounded more British than Southern.

"To the point, Mr. Nudger. I understand you've been asking questions about Ineida Mann."

To the point it would be. "True," Nudger said.

"Why?"

"Do you mean why isn't it any of your concern?"

Reckoner smiled. It was a nice smile, his handsome face seamed with deep laugh lines. A man like this could enhance his reputation as a nice guy even as he was pulling a knife from your back. All in the smile. "It is my concern," he said. "I'm interested in Ineida's career. She's a very sweet, very talented young woman."

He seemed to mean it about the talent, so Nudger decided to leave it alone.

Reckoner leaned slightly forward over the wide expanse of old desk. "You told Norman you're a private detective. I assume someone hired you in regard to Ineida. Would it be contrary to your professional code to reveal the name of your employer?"

"It would without my client's permission," Nudger said.

"Is Ineida in some sort of trouble? She isn't getting rich singing at Fat Jack's; I'm prepared to help her out financially if that has anything to do with her problem."

"She doesn't need financial assistance," Nudger assured Reckoner. "Actually I came here to ask you just what your relationship with her is, and what you think of her relationship with Willy Hollister."

Reckoner shrugged inside the elegant gray jacket. In the way of quality tailoring, it seemed to shrug with him, as if adopting the mood of whoever wore it were part of the bargain. "I just described my relationship with Ineida; she's a fine young person I'd like to help. I have the means to assist her in her singing career, so why shouldn't I do just that?"

"No reason not to," Nudger said. "If that's as far as your interest in her goes."

Reckoner leaned back and smiled, this time sagely and tolerantly. It made Nudger want to punch him. "Are you moralizing, Mr. Nudger?"

"Not at all. Only speculating. A pretty young girl, an older married man . . ."

"You're miles out of line, Nudger."

"I apologize if I've offended you. My work mostly takes me out of line. Sometimes I go weeks without even seeing the line."

"What would prompt you to suspect some sort of romantic involvement between Ineida and me?"

"At the risk of offending you again," Nudger said, "you must be aware that you have something of a reputation as a philanderer."

Reckoner stiffened, managed to look as indignant as a gray-bearded schnauzer whose food dish had suddenly been snatched away. "Ineida's virtually a child, Nudger. I don't molest children."

"She's a beautiful young woman," Nudger said. "I'll admit that she's naive in some areas, but a twenty-two-year-old girl is no longer a child in the view of a lot of people. Sometimes the wrong kind of people."

"I'm not one of the wrong kind," Reckoner said coldly. He stood up, letting his knuckles rest lightly on the desktop. It seemed the conversation was over.

Nudger also stood and buttoned his sport jacket. "You haven't told me what you think about Ineida seeing Willy Hollister."

"I see no evidence that Hollister is one of the wrong kind of people, either. Ineida's relationship with him is none of my business. Or yours."

Nudger idly picked up a cream-colored glass vase from a corner of the desk.

"Don't drop that," Reckoner said calmly but testily. "It's worth more than you might imagine."

"Looks ordinary enough," Nudger said.

"It's Bristol glass. It looks like ordinary milk glass, but hold it up to the light and you'll see a reddish glow in it."

Nudger held the vase up and tilted it toward the window; the milky glass did take on a transparency and glow a fiery red.

"Only the light shining through it will reveal the fire," Reckoner said.

"Very often," Nudger said, "that's true of people, too."

Reckoner shook his head almost sadly. "I was afraid you'd make that strained analogy."

He sat back down and busied himself with a stack of irregular-sized papers that looked like shipping invoices. His manner suggested that Nudger's presence was no longer important enough to acknowledge; enough time had been wasted on things trivial.

Nudger turned and saw that Norman was standing on the red carpet, holding the door open for him. Not a sound had been made; it was as if he'd been there in the office all the time and just now decided to become visible. He could sure move quietly on those tasseled moccasins. Some spooky guy.

Without speaking, he ushered Nudger through the shop to the street door and back out into the sunlight, noise, exhaust fumes, and heat of the twentieth century.

The sidewalk was heavily peopled by shoppers now; commerce was picking up along the block of small shops and restaurants. As Nudger stepped aside to avoid a determined-looking obese mother lugging a sour-faced infant, he saw that a woman was leaning against his parked car with her arms folded. She was lounging comfortably in a patient, waiting sort of way; if she'd been in uniform, Nudger would have assumed she was a cop waiting to greet him with an official smile, a lecture, and a parking ticket.

He didn't break stride. When he got closer he recognized her. Sandra Reckoner. Max's wife.

Her smile was warmer than a cop's official grimace as she straightened her long body and turned slightly to face him. She was built tall and rangy, like her husband, and was wearing dark slacks with tight cuffs and a crazily printed colorful blouse that had enough material under the arms to make her appear to have folded wings; if she ran fast enough into the wind, she might be able to fly.

She said, "I'm Sandra Reckoner, Mr. Nudger. We have things to talk about."

He shook hands with her lightly, sensing the strength in her long, lean fingers. She was wearing pink nail polish, a bulky antique ring, and a dull-gold bracelet that twined around her wrist like an affectionate snake.

"You've been talking with my husband," she told him. She had coarse, shoulder-length black hair flecked with gray, framing a narrow, bigboned face that should have been horsey-looking but wasn't. Her eyes, greenish-blue and amused, looked out with a candid directness, almost a sensuous dare, above her high cheekbones. This was an attractive woman living at ease with her forty-odd years, and her almost luminous health lent her a sexual vitality that hummed.

Nudger nodded, a bit awkwardly, still gauging the pull of her magnetism, testing the air for trouble. Certain women affected him that way initially. "I just left the antique shop," he confirmed.

"Now it's our turn to chat," Sandra Reckoner said. "I know a place where we can do that."

That sounded interesting to Nudger. He leaned to open the car door for her.

"We can walk," she told him.

He swallowed, nodded again, and followed her. Gee, those long legs moved lazily and smoothly beneath the silky material of her slacks. Rhythm, rhythm. He found it difficult to look away from them.

She paused for a moment at the corner, waiting for traffic to stop for a red light, then forged on ahead.

He almost got run over trying to keep up with her as they crossed the street.

XIII

Sandra Reckoner's long legs were still striding in Nudger's imagination as he sat across from her in a booth near the back of The Instrumental, a lounge they'd entered at the end of the block. It was in a rehabbed and converted two-story frame row house. She acted as though she was familiar with the place, a narrow, dim room decorated with musical instruments mounted on the walls and suspended by thin wires from the ceiling. A carpeted spiral staircase led up to another room where there were more tables. Nudger could see the shoes and pants legs of diners near where the stairway wound into the second floor.

A husky blond barmaid without a waist, wearing a floor-length print skirt and a melancholy expression, came out from behind the long bar and took their orders. Nudger asked for Seven-Up over ice; Sandra Reckoner nodded to the barmaid as if she knew her and asked for Scotch on the rocks. The barmaid went back behind the bar and did something that caused soft sax music to drift out from speakers hidden around the place; considerate of her, since the morning was young and they were the only downstairs customers.

"Kind of early for me to be drinking high-proof stuff," Nudger said, when their drinks were placed before them on cork coasters featuring superimposed photos of well-known jazz musicians. He sipped his Seven-Up and set the glass down smack on the grinning face of poor Pete Fountain.

"The hour makes no difference to me," Sandra said. "People pay too much attention to clocks. I drink when I need a drink, which is often." Nudger doubted that she was telling him she was an alcoholic. She showed no signs of the disease; she glowed with that disturbingly good health that upsets male libidos. "Oh, I get drunk now and then," she said suddenly. "I enjoy it. Getting a little goosed once in a while makes my life more acceptable to me."

"What in your life do you find hard to accept?" Nudger asked, knowing the answer.

"What you were talking to my husband about: Ineida Mann. And so many others like her." She took a pull of Scotch. "Hell, they all look alike. Ever noticed how young girls nowadays seem sort of mass-produced?"

"I have. I thought that might be because I'm getting older. Is that why we're here? So you can ask me about Ineida and Max?"

Sandra sipped her drink daintily now, aimed her amused eyes at him over the glass rim. "Mostly, that's why we're here. My husband's infidelities are nothing new to me. I think he's a victim of male menopause. Like a number of middle-aged men, he likes younger women."

"He shouldn't," Nudger said candidly.

She picked up the sincerity in his voice and smiled. "Thanks, Mr. Nudger; that lifts me up more than this drink." She cocked her head to the side and stared at him, as if suddenly her undivided attention had been captured. "What's your first name?"

"Aloysius. But everyone just calls me Nudger."

"Lucky you." She leaned away and draped a long arm over the back of the booth; there was something sweeping and elegant in the gesture. Something grand. "Well?"

"I think the answer is no."

Sandra laughed deep in her throat, throwing back her head and exposing large, perfectly aligned teeth that were slightly stained. She had a way of glancing out of the corner of her eye when she did that, reminding Nudger of a spirited thoroughbred filly tossing back its head. He again reflected that she shouldn't have been as attractive as she was; her appeal puzzled and intrigued him.

"Your husband, as far as I know, has never slept with Ineida Mann."

"How far do you know, Nudger?"

"Almost to the horizon. Are you well acquainted with Ineida?"

"No, not really. She's just another young face and body of the type Max seems to gather around him. Sometimes they respond to his advances and sometimes they don't. Let's face it, Nudger, a wife has a right to be suspicious when her husband is spending time with a woman named Ineida Mann. I know you've been asking questions about the girl; I figured you could tell me something about her."

"She isn't what she seems," Nudger said. "And I don't think she's at all interested in Max. She's involved with someone else."

"Who? That piano player, Hollister? What does that prove? She might take on more than one man in one night, for all I know. What kind of background does she have? How the hell did she come up with that schmucky stage name? Who the *fuck* is she?"

"She comes from a nice family"—Nudger almost choked

on his Seven-Up—"and she's more naive than she, and most of the people who see her perform, would like to believe. She's a blues singer; she wants to give the impression that she knows something about the hard knocks and pain she's describing in her lyrics."

"Are you telling me she's using all that heat just to try to sell a song?"

Nudger nodded.

"Her act's a good one, then," Sandra said. "She doesn't exactly come across the footlights as Polly Pure." She drained her Scotch, signaled with a crook of a long finger to the husky barmaid, who had her back turned to watch soundless TV but caught the signal in the backbar mirror. "You want another Seven-Up, Nudger? I'm buying."

"No, thanks. Too much carbonation this time of day will set off my stomach."

"What's the matter with your stomach?"

"Nerves."

"Then you're in the wrong business, aren't you?"

"You betcha." He watched as Sandra's drink was replaced by a fresh one. "Have I put your mind at ease?"

"Somewhat," she said. "But then, my mind is usually more or less at ease."

"It doesn't seem as if your situation warrants that enviable state of tranquillity," Nudger told her.

"Why not? Because the marital scales are out of balance? But they're not; I see to that. My response to Max's philandering is to enjoy my own infidelities, Nudger. I believe in vengeance through orgasm."

Nudger breathed in some carbonation bubbles through his nose, coughed, and lowered his glass. "That's a, er, fascinating philosophy."

She was smiling broadly now, toying, in control of the game. "Are you deeply involved with anyone, Nudger?"

"Very much so." He stared at the languid curve of her long arm, the play of bright flesh along her throat as she tilted back her head to sip her Scotch. "Well, fairly involved."

"Max doesn't know about my affairs. And he's not observant enough to suspect, much less find out; these days his thought processes occur well below the belt line. I like it that way; I do things for my satisfaction, not his dissatisfaction. That's the difference between my affairs and his. Nobody gets hurt my way. Everything's agreed on beforehand; no strings attached to either party. Freedom's an exhilarating experience."

"If there is such a thing."

"Oh, there is, Nudger." She worked on her drink some more, then suddenly set the glass down as if she'd lost interest in it. "So? Does my way of coping with my husband's infidelities interest you?"

"Do you mean interest me in a personal way?"

"Of course."

Nudger thought hard about Claudia. It was difficult to bring her features into sharp focus in his mind.

"There isn't necessarily anything wrong or cheap about lust, Nudger."

"Hm, that's something to think about."

Smiling, she stood up, picking up the bar check to pay on her way out. "Then think about it."

Nudger watched her settle with the blond barmaid and walk out without looking back at him. He knew she was aware that he was staring; he could tell that by the measured cadence of her long-legged stride.

He sipped his Seven-Up. It tasted flat, now that Sandra

Reckoner had gone. Instead of finishing his drink, he sat silently in the cool lounge, rotating his glass on its damp coaster. Thinking.

Thinking.

XIV

Though plenty of interested parties had warned Nudger to stay away from Ineida Collins, everyone had neglected to tell him to give wide berth to Willy Hollister. After Nudger left his unsettling verbal joust with Sandra Reckoner, it was Hollister who claimed his interest.

Hollister lived on Rue St. Francois, within a few blocks of Ineida. Their apartments were similar. Hollister's was the end unit of a low, tan brick-and-stucco building that sat almost flush with the sidewalk. What yard there was had to be in the rear. Through the glossy-green low branches of a huge magnolia tree, Nudger saw some of the raw cedar fencing, weathered almost black, that sectioned off the back premises into private courtyards.

Hollister might be home, sleeping after his late-night gig at Fat Jack's. Nudger rapped on the wooden door three times, then casually leaned toward it and listened, trying to blank out the street sounds from his mind.

He heard no sound from inside. He straightened and turned his head slightly, looking around; no one on the street seemed to be paying the slightest attention to him. After a few seconds' wait, he idly gave the doorknob a twist.

It rotated all the way, giving a sharp click. The door opened about six inches on its own, because of weight and balance. Sort of an invitation. Nudger pushed the door open the rest of the way and stepped quietly inside.

The apartment no doubt came furnished; it had that hodgepodge, multi-user look about it. The furniture was old but not too worn; some of it probably had antique value. Nudger thought the building's owner and Max Reckoner ought to get together and strike a deal. There was a milky-white vase on a shelf, not so unlike the vase Nudger had admired in Reckoner's office.

The floor in Hollister's apartment was dull hardwood where it showed around the borders of a faded blue carpet. Muted sunlight caught the faint fuzziness of dust on the wood surface and on the fancy corner molding; Hollister wasn't the best of housekeepers. From where Nudger stood he could see into the bedroom. The bed was unmade but empty.

The living room was dim. The wooden shutters on its windows were closed, allowing slanted light to filter in through narrow slits. Most of the illumination in the room came from the bedroom and a short hall that led to a bathroom, then to a small kitchen and sliding glass doors that opened to the courtyard.

Wondering if he was actually alone, Nudger glanced around nervously, called, "Mr. Hollister? Gallup Poll!"

No answer. Only buzzing silence. Fine.

Nudger walked around the living room for a few minutes, examining the contents of drawers, picking up some sealed mail that turned out to be an insurance pitch and a utility bill. He was still haunted by the worrisome knowledge that Hollister wasn't the type to go away and leave his apartment unlocked. Especially not after his run-in with Sam Judman.

As he entered the bedroom, he heard a noise from outside the curtained window, which was open about four inches for ventilation. It was a dull thunking sound he thought he recognized. He went to the window, parted the breeze-swayed gauzy white curtains, and bent low to peer outside.

The window looked out on the courtyard. What Nudger saw confirmed his guess about the sound. It was made by a shovel knifing into soft earth. Willy Hollister was in the garden, digging. Nudger crouched low so he could see better, brushing a gossamer, caressing curtain away like a web from his face.

Hollister was planting rosebushes. They were young plants, but they already had red and white buds on them. Hollister had started on the left with the red roses and was alternating colors. He was planting half a dozen bushes and was working on the fifth plant, which lay with its roots wrapped in burlap beside the waiting, freshly dug hole.

Hollister was on both knees on the ground, using his hands to scoop some dirt back into the hole. He was carefully shaping a small dome over which to spread the soon-to-be-exposed roots before adding more loose earth. He knew how to plant rosebushes, all right, and he was doing his best to ensure that these would live.

Nudger's stomach went into a series of spasms as Hollister stood up and glanced at the apartment as if he'd sensed someone's presence. The musician wiped one of the rolled-up sleeves of his tan shirt across his perspiring forehead. He must have been working hard for quite a while; he stood angled forward at the waist, like a man whose back ached. For a few seconds he seemed to debate about whether to return to the apartment. Then he absently massaged one of his corded forearms, picked up the long-handled shovel, and began digging the sixth and final hole.

Letting out a long, hissing breath, Nudger drew back from the open window and stood up straight. He'd go out by the front door now, then walk around to the courtyard and call Hollister's name, as if he'd just arrived and gotten no answer at the front door and decided to check the courtyard. He wanted to talk to Hollister, to probe for the man's own version of his past.

As Nudger was leaving the bedroom, he noticed a stack of pale blue envelopes on the dresser, beside a comb-and-brush set monogrammed with Hollister's initials. The envelopes were held together by a fat rubber band. Nudger saw the Beulah Street address penned neatly in black ink in a corner of the top envelope.

Here was one of the nasty aspects of his work; ends justifying means, gain outweighing scruples. How much of himself did he lose each time he did something like this?

But he paused for only a few seconds before he picked up the envelopes and slipped them into his pocket. Then he left Hollister's apartment the same way he'd entered.

There was no point in talking to Hollister now. It would be foolish to place himself in the apartment at the approximate time of the disappearance of the stack of letters written by Ineida Collins.

He walked up Rue St. Francois for several blocks, then took a cab to his hotel. Though the morning was still more muggy than hot, the cab's air conditioner was on high and the interior was near freezing. The letters seemed to grow heavier in Nudger's pocket, and to glow with a kind of warmth that gave no comfort.

XV

Nudger had Room Service bring up a two-egg cheese omelet and a glass of milk. He sat at the desk in his hotel room with his early lunch, his customary meal that had a soothing effect on his nervous stomach, and ate slowly as he read Ineida Collins' letters to Hollister. He understood now why they had felt warm inside his pocket. The love affair was, from Ineida's point of view at least, as soaring and serious as such an affair can get. Nudger again felt cheapened by his crass invasion of Ineida's privacy. These were thoughts meant to be shared by no other than writer and recipient, thoughts not meant to be tramped through by a middle-aged detective not under the spell of love.

On the other hand, he told himself, there was no way for him to know what the letters contained *until* he read them and determined that he shouldn't have. Once he'd stolen the letters, he was caught up in logic in another context. This was again the sort of professional quandary he got himself into frequently but never got used to.

The last letter, the one with the latest postmark, was the

most revealing and made the tacky side of Nudger's profession seem almost worthwhile. Here was the nugget of pertinent, illuminating information he sought—a justification for his actions. Ineida Collins was planning to run away with Willy Hollister; he told her he loved her and that they would be married. Then, after the fact, they would return to New Orleans and inform friends and relatives of the blessed union. It all seemed so quaint, Nudger thought, and not very believable unless you happened to be twenty-two and lovestruck and had lived Ineida Collins' sheltered existence.

Ineida also referred in the last letter to something important she had to tell Hollister. Nudger could guess what that important bit of information was. That she was Ineida Collins and she was David Collins' daughter and she was rich, and that she was oh so glad that Hollister hadn't known about her until that moment. Because that meant he wanted her for her own true self alone. Ah, love! It made a PI's business go round.

He refolded the letter, replaced it in its envelope, and dropped it onto the desk.

Nudger tried to finish his omelet but couldn't. It had become cool as he'd read the heated letters. He wasn't really hungry anyway, and his stomach had reached a tolerable level of discomfort. He knew it was time to report to Fat Jack. After all, the man had hired him to uncover information, not to keep to himself.

Nudger slipped the rubber band back around the stack of letters, snapped it, and stood up. He considered having the letters placed in the hotel safe, but the security of any hotel safe was questionable. A paper napkin bearing the Hotel Majestueux's gold fleur-de-lis logo lay next to his half-eaten omelet. He wrapped the envelopes in the napkin and dropped the bundle into the wastebasket by the desk.

The maid wasn't due back in the room until tomorrow morning, and it was unlikely that anyone would think Nudger would throw away such important letters. And the sort of person who would bother to search a wastebasket would search everywhere else and find the letters anyway.

He placed the tray with his dishes on it in the hall outside his door, hung the "Do Not Disturb" sign on the knob, and left to see Fat Jack McGee.

On the sidewalk outside the hotel, he heard his name called. At first he thought it was the old doorman, but when Nudger turned, the doorman studiously looked away from him, his face blank and composed in a way that alerted Nudger.

A short, paunchy man in a rumpled brown suit approached Nudger from where he'd been waiting in the deep cool shadow of the building. He had unruly receding hair, a chubby, jowly face, and he was smiling a rigor-mortis sort of smile. Nudger wasn't surprised when he flashed a shield. He said, still smiling, "I'm Sergeant Chambers, Mr. Nudger. How about you should follow me down to the district station house so Captain Livingston can have a chat with you?"

"How about you should give me a choice?" Nudger said.

Chambers shook his head no, then cocked it sharply to the side. He had gum in his mouth; he began to chew it slowly with a gum chewer's peculiar insolence, not letting the effort interfere with his toothy smile. "Sorry, can't do that."

Nudger sighed. "Okay. I'm parked down the block."

"I know." Chambers popped his gum; it sounded like a gunshot. "My partner's parked right behind your car."

Nudger began to walk. Chambers fell into step beside and slightly behind him. The old doorman continued to be a nonperson, "See, Hear, and Speak No Evil" all rolled into one. In his very practical world, there was safety in anonymity. Right now, Nudger wished that philosophy were his own. If it were, he wouldn't be on his way to the station house with rumpled, gum-popping Chambers to clash with officialdom.

If if's were skiffs, as his ex-wife Eileen used to tell him sternly, *we all would sailors be.* Nudger was never sure what she meant by that. He thought that might have been her way of trying to get him to join the Navy.

"Why does Livingston want to talk with me?" he asked, as they approached the parked cars.

Chambers shrugged. "I dunno. I guess you been making waves." He touched Nudger's arm lightly to stop him and held open the rear door of a gray-blue sedan. "We might as well all go in the squad car," he said. "Be chummier. Save you gasoline."

He got into the back of the car after Nudger and settled down heavily into the upholstery; he smelled like Juicy Fruit. The driver, a broad-shouldered man with a fuzzy reddish bald spot on the crown of his head, didn't look back or say anything as he started the car and drove toward the station house.

XVI

Chambers ushered Nudger into Livingston's office, then withdrew without saying anything; Nudger heard the loud pop of gum on the other side of the door just after it closed.

The first thing he noticed about Livingston's office was that it was large. The wall behind the desk was mostly windows looking out over a depressed, gloomy section of New Orleans. Which puzzled Nudger for a moment, because it was a sunny day. Then he saw that the gloom was the result of a dirty film over the windows; it was all interior gloom.

The office was plush; there were two cream-colored velour chairs angled near the desk, police-uniform-blue carpet, and something that looked like a liquor cabinet in a far corner. The walls were paneled halfway up. Real paneling, not the plastic laminated stuff. Livingston sat behind his desk, the top of which was bare except for a green desk pad, some pencils, and a large clear glass vase that was crammed full of tall, bushy flowers of a kind that Nudger didn't recognize. He wondered if Livingston had a secretary, and if it was her job to supply fresh flowers for the vase every morning. He was the type.

"Sit down, Nudger," Livingston said brusquely.

"And good morning to you," Nudger told him, lowering himself into one of the creamy velour chairs. It was sneaky comfortable, the kind of chair that might not lull you into dozing, but that you'd find you didn't want to stand up out of when it was time to rise. He glanced around. "The New Orleans Police Department treats its captains royally."

Livingston peered at him around the bushy flowers, like a fox peeking out from deep cover. "Not really. You're just used to the low-rent ratholes private cops operate out of."

"I can see it was mostly tact that got you where you are."

"It was hard work," Livingston corrected. "And instinct. A talent for sniffing out trouble."

"And I smell like trouble?"

"You absolutely reek of it, Nudger."

"I'm sure you didn't call me down here just to get a whiff of me," Nudger said, shifting his weight in the soft chair so Livingston would have to crane his neck to continue watching him around the desk flora.

"It's been brought to my attention," Livingston said, "that just prior to our conversation in your hotel room, you were out of town for several days."

Nudger nodded. "Business."

"What kind of business?"

"The private kind, I'm afraid."

"Concerning the job you're doing here in New Orleans?"

"Partly."

"Then your business isn't so private that it isn't my business, too." Livingston rolled his chair to the side to get a better angle of vision across the desk, save himself from a stiff neck. "Tell me about it."

Nudger decided it was time to give something to Livingston; if he didn't, Livingston would take and keep on
taking. It was the nature of the animal. "I'll tell you whatever I can," he said.

"Then it should be easy for you. I only want to know
three things: Where did you go? Who did you see? What did
you find out?"

"I went to Cleveland, Kansas City, Chicago, and St.
Louis. I talked to people connected with the jazz scene."

"Talked to them about what?" Livingston asked, when
Nudger didn't continue.

"Willy Hollister."

Livingston sat back and toyed with one of the sharp yellow pencils on the desk, adroitly holding its center still and
rotating the ends, as if it were a compass needle that might
point out the truth. "Hollister. The piano player over at Fat
Jack's club?"

Nudger nodded.

"And what did you find out?"

"About Hollister?"

The pencil stopped being a compass; it became a gun,
aimed at Nudger as if Livingston itched to fill him fatally
with #2 lead. "Who else would I mean, Nudger?"

"Maybe David Collins. I found out some things about
him."

"Let's stay with Hollister."

"Why not Collins?"

Livingston said nothing, looked uncomfortable, waited.
There was a new hard glint in his slanted little eyes. It suggested that here was a man who, if pushed, would push
back hard. He was a tough cop, even though he looked like
a conniving little wimp. Nudger knew it was time to get
cooperative.

"Hollister makes women disappear," he said.

Livingston was unimpressed by this vague revelation. "He does magic? I thought he was a musician." His voice had taken on the same sharp flintiness as his eyes.

"With a certain type of woman, he does magic," Nudger said. "They fall hard for him, have a passionate affair, then drop out of sight."

"You're saying Hollister has something to do with their disappearances?" Livingston asked. A coplike question, to the point and phrased to suggest the answer.

"There's nothing to indicate that," Nudger said. He decided to give Hollister the benefit of the doubt in this conversation with Livingston. After all, Nudger hadn't any real proof that the man had done anything the slightest bit illegal. "Maybe his women just get tired of being around all that ego," he said. "They might be surprised when they're caught in a love triangle: Hollister, the woman, and Hollister."

Livingston seemed to decide not to probe deeper. He leaned back, hiding for a moment behind his vase of foliage. Nudger could see his pointy little ears through the green stems. Livingston was gauging the situation; at this juncture, he might not want to know too much about Willy Hollister's love life. After all, there were people who might ask *him* questions.

"You're going to get your nose badly bent, poking it in the wrong places," Livingston said. "What were you doing in the Golden Oldens shop earlier today?"

Nudger shrugged. "I like old goodies."

"Goodies like Sandra Reckoner?"

"She's not so old," Nudger said. "Not a worm hole in her."

"Don't be so sure. I hear she gets turned on in the oddest ways by the oddest people." Livingston gave the sly, nasty smile of a pornographer or a censor.

"Why are you warning me again not to nose around?" Nudger asked. "Didn't we pretty much cover that subject in my hotel room?"

"Not completely. I want to make sure you understand something, Nudger. There are certain kinds of situations where I can't help you."

Nudger wasn't sure if he did understand. Was Livingston jerking strings for his own self-serving reasons, or was he actually at least obliquely concerned about Nudger's welfare? Was he the snide little bought cop he appeared to be, or was he something else, something harder to classify?

"Even strong swimmers drown now and then," Livingston said. "They do it by getting in over their heads when there's no lifeguard around."

Nudger wondered what was going on. Every cop he knew seemed to be speaking in metaphors all of a sudden. "You should meet my friend Hammersmith," he said.

"Who's he?"

"Oh, just a guy I know back in St. Louis."

"Back in St. Louis is where you oughta be."

"That seems to be the prevailing logic."

Livingston stood up; it wasn't easy to catch behind that big desk. "Keep yourself out of trouble, Nudger. My men have better things to do than tail you around the city."

Nudger got up out of the creamy velour chair, listening to his knees pop; he was getting old—like Billy Weep. No, he corrected himself, Billy wasn't getting older now. Nudger hadn't seen any point in telling Livingston about Weep's death. He looked out the window again at the world made gloomy by what went on inside Livingston's office, the way Livingston's world was clouded by what went on inside his head.

"What are you staring at?" Livingston asked.

"Nothing in particular," Nudger told him. "Nice suit. Wool?"

Livingston said nothing; Nudger left the office in silence, closing the door behind him softly. Wool, Nudger decided. A fox in sheep's clothing, that was Livingston. What was going on in his cunning little mind?

Out on the sidewalk, Nudger paused. His stomach was rumbling, threatening to make itself felt in ways unpleasant. He reached for his roll of spearmint-flavored antacid tablets.

An explosion behind him made him jump and whirl.

It was Chambers, popping his gum. The scent of Juicy Fruit wafted to Nudger.

The detective grinned at him, holding the pale wad of gum between his front teeth so it was visible when he smiled, like a kid proving to his mother that he hasn't swallowed it. "Give you a lift back to your hotel?" he offered, motioning with his head toward where the blue-gray sedan that had brought Nudger to the station house was parked across the street.

Nudger nodded. "Why not?"

Chambers winced. "That's a terrible philosophy. Better to ask yourself why." Then he shrugged. "On the other hand, people who ask themselves 'Why not?' keep me in a job." *Pop!* went the gum.

"They're both tough questions," Nudger said.

He broke the seal on a fresh role of antacid tablets and he and Chambers walked across the street side by side. Juicy Fruit and Spearmint.

XVII

After Chambers had dropped him off at the Hotel Majestueux, Nudger was surprised to notice a slip of folded white paper in his message box behind the desk. He asked the towering desk clerk for it, unfolded it, and read:

Mr. Nudger,
  I'm sorry I missed you. I'll try to contact you again as soon as possible. It's important that we talk.
                                          Marilyn Eeker

Nudger examined the paper. It was cheap unlined notepaper, folded once and deeply creased as if a thumbnail had been run hard across it. The handwriting was in pale blue ink, concise and feminine, and at a slight downward angle to the top edge of the paper.

"When was this delivered?" Nudger asked the desk clerk.

"About an hour ago," the clerk said, jackknifing his long body downward over the desk to pencil figures into a ledger book. He was a busy man; taking time to talk with Nudger was obviously an imposition.

"Did the woman say anything?" Nudger asked.

Not looking up, the tall clerk said, "Just told me to please put this in Mr. Nudger's message box." He began applying pencil point to paper.

"What did she look like?"

"Oh, smallish—petite, I guess you'd say—blond, in her forties, kinda pretty. Seemed in a hurry."

Nudger searched his mental file, couldn't imagine who the woman might be. He couldn't remember ever hearing the name Marilyn Eeker.

The clerk scratched his gray head and began to struggle with a miniature calculator. Nudger left him in the hands of science and went up to his room.

The New Orleans phone directory listed only one Eeker. Joseph Eeker. Nudger phoned his number, asked to speak to him, and was immediately connected. It was all so easy Nudger knew it wouldn't bear fruit.

He was right. Joseph Eeker was seventy-nine years old and had never heard of Marilyn Eeker and didn't want to hear of her again. Nudger apologized for being such a bother and hung up. He would have to wait for Marilyn Eeker to come to him. He hoped she didn't represent someone he owed.

His conversation with Livingston, and his time cooped up in the car with Chambers and his ominously silent partner, had made Nudger perspire. He washed his face with cold water, then put on a fresh shirt and went back downstairs and outside.

He drove the red subcompact in the direction of Fat Jack's club, wondering why Livingston hadn't mentioned his entering and leaving Hollister's apartment. It could be that police surveillance had already been called off at that time and Livingston simply didn't know about Nudger's being at Hollister's. Livingston was speaking the truth when he'd said his men had better things to do than trail Nudger. The New Orleans police force was as overworked as any other police department. Or it could be that Livingston knew about Nudger's going to Hollister's and deliberately hadn't mentioned it, playing his cards close to his little fox vest. Another possibility was that Livingston's man had seen Nudger at Hollister's and assumed a conversation had occurred, and Livingston hadn't thought the visit worth mentioning.

Nudger decided to quit worrying about Livingston. Trying to analyze the motives of a cop like that was the sort of thing that ate holes in stomachs. He didn't need that.

He parked the car, then pushed in through the door of Fat Jack's, leaving the heat and brightness of outside for the cool dimness of the club.

The bartender—not the young unflappable one, but an elderly gray guy with a polka-dot bow tie—told Nudger that Fat Jack was out. Nobody knew for sure when he'd be back; he might not return until the evening, when business started picking up, or he might have just strolled over to the Magnolia Blossom for a croissant and coffee and would be back any minute.

Nudger sat at the end of the bar, nursing a beer he didn't really want, and waited. He watched the bartender, who had the air of a natty dresser despite the wrinkled white apron tied around his waist, get things ready behind the bar for the night. It was almost as if the long bar were a barricade, and he was making sure there was plenty of ammunition to deal with an imminent siege. He arranged bottles on the backbar so he could reach them easily, counted gleaming upside-down glasses as if they were artillery shells. It looked to Nudger like a boring job, nothing like sitting awake in a parked car all night waiting for a client's errant spouse to leave a motel room.

Marty Sievers walked in from the back room. He stood for a while watching some of the early customers wander in and be shown to tables. He was wearing the same conservative brown suit he'd had on the first time Nudger saw him. Mr. Average; if they built an Everyman robot, it would look like Sievers. When he caught sight of Nudger, he walked over and stood next to him at the bar.

"Looks like it's going to be a busy night," Nudger said.

"It will be. Hollister makes for busy nights. In fact, we've had a busy month." The bartender brought him over a glass of what looked like pure club soda over ice. Maybe Perrier water. Sievers raised the glass in an amiable toast, smiling at Nudger, and sipped.

"Do you happen to know Max Reckoner?" Nudger asked.

"Sure, the guy who owns the antique shops. He's a regular. So's his wife Sandra, but she doesn't come in as often as Max."

"I've heard Max does his hunting in here," Nudger said.

"Hunting?"

"Yeah. Max and Cupid."

Sievers gave him a level look. "I don't talk about the customers, Nudger. It's bad business."

"I could get my information from Fat Jack if you don't want to tell me."

"Maybe you should do that."

"It has to do with the welfare of the club."

The cash-register bell sounded behind the bar. Or was it Sievers' heart?

"There can't be any business, good or bad, if there's no

business at all," Sievers said with perfect logic. If he hadn't been Green Beret, he'd have been Junior Achievement. "It's true that Max likes the young ones."

"How does Sandra react to that?"

Sievers took another sip of his unblemished drink and shrugged. "She knows about it, but what can she do if she doesn't want to leave the guy? My impression is she's just waiting around for him to get through middle-aged madness and settle back down."

Middle-aged madness. Nudger wondered if he might be suffering from that. "Does Sandra have affairs of her own, to compensate?" he asked.

"I don't know," Sievers said, a bit sharply. Nudger wondered if there had ever been any relationship between him and Sandra Reckoner. He decided not to ask Sievers about that; he wouldn't get an answer that meant anything, and Sievers would probably stop talking altogether.

A busty redheaded waitress wearing a Fat Jack's T-shirt bounced by carrying an empty tray. Inspiration. "Has Max scored with any of the help here?" Nudger asked.

"I agreed to tell you about the customers, not the employees," Sievers said.

"You're going to make me travel the long route to the same destination," Nudger told him. "It could cost you a lot."

"Maybe."

"If you tell me, nobody will know where I got the information."

Sievers ran his finger along the rim of his glass, listening to the high-pitched, faint whining sound, and thought about that. "Okay," he said finally. "You're supposed to be a confidential investigator."

"I am," Nudger said seriously. "It's what my job is all about."

"Judy Villanova," Sievers said. He motioned with a slight movement of his hand toward a frail blond waitress at the end of the bar who was loading her tray with drinks.

Nudger watched as she carried the frosty mugs of beer to a table where four businessman types sat. She had a delicate pale face that wasn't large enough for her overly made-up blue eyes. Her dark-stockinged thighs, though curvaceous, didn't fill out the legs of her shorts, and her T-shirt might have been several sizes too large for her. She looked like a teenager playing grown-up.

"How old is she?" Nudger asked.

"Twenty-seven. She's married and has a daughter. She works here part-time while she's going for a psychology degree at Loyola University."

"What time does she get off work tonight?"

"Nine o'clock. This is her short night; she's got an early class tomorrow." Sievers was frowning; he was a closed-mouthed guy and loyal to his troops. He obviously didn't like telling Nudger about one of his waitresses. "Judy is a good girl—woman. Whatever went on between her and Max happened over a year ago."

"I won't upset her any more than necessary," Nudger assured him.

"I'm not sure her husband knows about her and Max," Sievers said. He really did seem concerned.

The phone behind the bar rang, and the bartender answered it, then held the receiver out in a silent signal that meant the call was for Sievers.

Carrying his drink with him, Sievers excused himself from Nudger's company and moved toward the swing-gate near the far end of the bar. Nudger watched him talk for a few minutes on the phone, then hang up and disappear in the direction of the kitchen.

The bartender set another round of drinks on the stainless-steel section of bar near the taps, for Judy Villanova to load onto her tray. She sure did have a skinny, almost emaciated-looking body. She was so frail, almost ethereal. Nudger turned his attention to his drink. Max Reckoner was probably the kind of guy who liked to crush flowers.

After an hour, the bartender, whose name Nudger had found out was Mattingly, began blatantly staring at him every once in a while. Slow time of the day or not, Nudger was occupying a bar stool and had an obligation.

And maybe Mattingly was right; a certain protocol was necessary to preserve the world from chaos. Nudger was about to give in to the weighty responsibility of earning his place at the bar by ordering another drink he didn't want when Fat Jack appeared through the dimness like a light-footed obese spirit in a white vested suit.

He saw Nudger, smiled his fat man's beaming smile, and veered toward him, diamond rings and gold jewelry flashing fire beneath pale coat sleeves, a large diamond stickpin in his biblike tie. Glint, glint. He was a vision of sartorial immensity.

"We need to talk," Nudger told him.

"That's easy enough," Fat Jack said. "My office, hey?" He led the way, making Nudger feel somewhat like a pilot fish trailing a whale. Fat Jack had some kind of expensive cologne on today that smelled faintly of lemon. For an instant it made Nudger think of the lemon-oil scent in Reckoner's antique shop.

When they were settled in Fat Jack's office, Nudger said, "I came across some letters Ineida wrote to Hollister."

"Came across?"

Nudger shrugged. "She and Hollister plan to run away together, get married."

Fat Jack raised his eyebrows so high Nudger was afraid they might become detached. "Hollister ain't the marrying kind, Nudger."

"What kind is he?"

"I don't want to answer that."

"Maybe Ineida and Hollister will elope and live happily—"

"Stop!" Fat Jack interrupted him. He leaned forward over his desk, wide forehead glistening. "When are they planning on leaving?"

"I don't know. The letters didn't say."

"You gotta find out, Nudger."

"I could ask. But Captain Livingston wouldn't approve."

"Livingston has talked with you?"

"Twice. In my hotel room, and this morning in his office. Both times the thrust of the conversation was the same. He wants me to butt out. He assured me he had my best interests at heart."

Fat Jack appeared thoughtful. He swiveled in his chair and switched on the auxiliary window air conditioner. Its breeze stirred the papers on the desk, ruffled his graying, gingery hair. "I'm sure Hollister doesn't know who Ineida really is," Fat Jack said. "I'm also sure he doesn't love her; it ain't in the way he looks at her."

"You could be wrong about that."

"Maybe, but I doubt it. Why do you suppose he wants to marry her?"

"Maybe he found out how much she's worth."

"Not a chance of that. Unless she told him."

"She didn't tell him," Nudger said. "She's saving the big surprise for her wedding night."

"Humph!" Fat Jack said. "What do you think happened to those other women?"

"I think we both know," Nudger said.

Fat Jack sat silently and perspired. He knew, all right, but he didn't want to talk about it. As if rendering it into words would move it out of the realm of speculation and into the world of cold facts.

"Hollister likes to be in love," Nudger said, "and then he consciously denies himself the women he loves and possesses, feeding a loneliness and agony that surface in his music and lend it the stamp of blues greatness. It's a deliberate personal sacrifice for his art, the only way he can give his music the insane, tragic dimension that makes it his alone. The ultimate in the suffering artist. The problem is that the women he loves and leaves are never seen again."

Fat Jack wiped his forehead with the palm of his hand, then examined his fingers as if checking for blood. After a while he said, "God help me, Nudger, I can understand that. Hey, I don't approve of it, but the musician—the artist in me, old sleuth—can understand it."

Nudger knew what Fat Jack meant; the big man was a world-class musician who'd sacrificed bone-deep for his art. Sacrifice was part of the gig. The difference was that maybe Willy Hollister was sacrificing people, and Fat Jack was horrified that Ineida might join their growing number.

"Where was Hollister between four and six o'clock two nights ago?" Nudger asked.

Fat Jack rubbed his jowl where it flowed over his white collar. "At five he did his set here at the club, and he was around here till at least six. Why?"

"Billy Weep was killed between those times."

Fat Jack shook his head. "It isn't likely Hollister could have killed Billy and made it back to town here in time for work. Possible, but it would take some tight planning and an airline that flew on time. I say he had nothing to do with Billy's death, which is some relief."

Nudger had to agree with Fat Jack. Death and taxes were sure, but airline departures were something else.

"What now?" Fat Jack asked. "A talk with Ineida?"

"I don't think that would change anything," Nudger said. "It just might hurry things along."

Fat Jack sighed, tapped meaty knuckles on the desk. "You're right, she wouldn't believe anything we told her about Hollister."

"And we have no proof. Whatever we told her might not be true."

"I'd heard you were an optimist," Fat Jack said. *Pat, pat,* went his knuckles on the desk. Each time he moved his hand, his ring sent a bright spot of reflected light dancing across a wall, a live thing trapped in two dimensions.

"What about laying all this out for her father?" Nudger asked.

Fat Jack's eyes actually rolled in terror. "No, no! He mustn't know she's gotten in this position working here at the club while I'm supposed to be looking out for her. Hey, there's no telling what Collins would do. To Hollister, to any of us." He seemed to consider the possibilities for a moment, then rolled his eyes again and said, "God, no, don't go to Collins."

Nudger thought Fat Jack had made himself clear on that point. "Do you have any other ideas?" he asked.

"Monitor the situation," Fat Jack said. "And I'll do the same while Hollister and Ineida are here at the club. Meanwhile, keep trying to find out more about Hollister; maybe if we get some dirt on him we can convince him to leave Ineida alone, do his gig, and then move on."

"We're talking about murder here," Nudger reminded him.

"And maybe murder-to-be," Fat Jack said. "We gotta look out for our own skins in this situation."

Fat Jack had a persuasive argument there, thought potential victim-to-be Nudger.

"Hey, we got a right to live," Fat Jack said with deep conviction.

"Everything alive has that," Nudger told him. "But look what happens."

XVIII

Nudger returned to his hotel room after leaving Fat Jack's, where he sat on the edge of the bed, stared at the telephone, and listened to the resonant thrumming of elevator cables in an adjacent shaft. It was a hollow, forlorn sound, an echo of isolation. Distant train whistles had nothing on elevator cables when it came to loneliness.

He knew why he wanted to call Claudia. He missed her suddenly, achingly, and he realized that he hadn't been away from her for any appreciable length of time or distance since they'd met. But that wasn't the real reason he needed to talk with her.

He looked at his watch. Almost four o'clock. She might not be home from the school by now; calling her would be a gamble. She had a tangle of traffic to fight on Highway 40 in her long drive in from the county.

He decided not to wait, and pulled the phone over to his lap to punch out the switchboard number for direct long distance.

On the second ring, Claudia answered her phone.

"Is something wrong?" she asked, when she realized it was Nudger.

"There's always something wrong," he said. "That's what keeps me working at least sporadically."

She caught something in his voice, paused. "How come you called?" Wily woman.

"I love you. I miss you. I wanted to hear your voice and for you to hear mine."

"It's just like you to get homesick, Nudger, but not at all like you to admit it." The phone line sizzled and crackled in Nudger's ear. He waited. "Are you becoming involved with Ineida Studd?"

"That's Ineida Mann and you know it. And no, I'm not getting involved with her in the way you suggest." Nudger was surprised by her intuition; she was on target but off the mark. "Ineida is a tragic, naive child poised on the edge of the abyss; not my idea of a sex object."

"I'm sure your interest in her is strictly fatherly."

"Grandfatherly," Nudger said.

"Last time we talked you described it as avuncular."

"So I did."

He could hear Claudia breathing into the phone. Claudia and phones; he had met her over the phone, fallen in love with her via electronic impulse. "I trust you, Nudger." She didn't tell him that lightly, he knew.

Nudger thought it best not to say anything. He heard a hollow, rolling sound on the line. It took him a few seconds to identify it as thunder.

"It's going to storm in St. Louis," Claudia said. "It'll cool things off. Is it hot there?"

"Hot as the music; not a hint of relief. This is an unreal place, as exotic as Zanzibar. It's so swampy here they inter their dead aboveground. The cemeteries look like miniature cities without windows or traffic."

"They buried your friend Billy Weep today. I saw it on the television news in the school lounge when I was at lunch. Benjamin Harrison Jefferson."

"What?"

"That was Billy Weep's real name. Didn't you know that?"

"No. He told me it was something else, a long time ago."

"They showed part of the service on the news. A man named Rush read a eulogy. And somebody played a blues number on the saxophone. It was sadder than a funeral march."

"He wasn't laid out at the funeral parlor for very long," Nudger said.

"I don't think he was laid out at all. He died indigent. The musicians' union paid for his burial."

"Was there anything else on the news about him? Such as who might have killed him?"

"No."

Nudger wasn't surprised. The living weren't particularly interested anymore in Billy Weep, probably hadn't been since he'd stopped making music that saddened them but reminded them they were alive. Nudger stared out the window at the soft, slanted early evening light. Painters and photographers lived for this time of day; it was too bad the world really wasn't the way it appeared in such a light.

"Billy Weep's death is connected with what's going on in New Orleans, isn't it?" Claudia said.

"I think so."

"Are you . . . being careful?"

"More than is necessary." He knew that she understood

his caution was for both of them. She held her silence. Their wordless mutual understanding was more of a declaration of love than if either of them had professed love. Their relationship had evolved into this while neither of them was watching. That was the trap people fell into.

"Are you in any kind of imminent danger, Nudger?"

"Sure I am. And I'm scared. But that's the way of my half-assed occupation."

"You're always honest, anyway."

The dark worm of conscience writhed in Nudger.

"We're running up your phone bill," Claudia said. "Are you on an expense account?"

"I'm told that I am, but what I'm told and reality in this city seldom seem to match. It's been that way since I've been down here. Maybe it's something in the grits."

"The rain's started here now; it's blowing in and getting the floor wet. I'd better go close the window."

"Are you trying to get rid of me?"

"I'm trying not to need you so much. You and the mop."

"I might call you again tomorrow around this time," Nudger told her.

"Or you might not. Either way, I'll be here."

Nudger hung up the phone, replaced it on the night-stand, and sat gazing at it. There was something undeniably maudlin in such interdependence, he thought. He had never felt that way even in the early days of his marriage with Eileen. But then he had divorced Eileen.

His digestive tract let it be known that he'd thought about Eileen. She and it had never gotten along well. Their relationship had been conducive to ulcers, not Eileen's.

If he was going to mull over women who disturbed, he might as well check on the latest addition. He picked up the receiver again and punched out the number for the desk.

"Are there any messages for Nudger, Room three-oh-four?" he asked.

The desk clerk mumbled in a way that suggested that there were never any messages for anyone, but said that he would check. The phone downstairs clattered as he set it down.

Nudger waited.

"Yes, sir," a somewhat surprised voice said after a few minutes. "A phone message marked three o'clock. From a Miss Marilyn Eeker."

Nudger gripped the receiver tighter and pressed it hard to his ear. "Well, what does it say?"

"It says she's sorry she missed you again and will call or come by whenever she can."

Nudger relaxed his grip on the receiver. He wished now he hadn't called the desk. He was right where he'd been before the call, only more puzzled and anxious.

"Anything else, sir?" There was alertness and respect in the clerk's voice now. A guest who got messages at the Majestueux commanded that.

"No. And thanks." Nudger hung up, and unglued his fingers the rest of the way from the phone.

He chewed a couple of antacid tablets and lay on his back on the bed, one hand toying with the phone cord and the other absently massaging his uneasy stomach, and thought about it raining in St. Louis. At least it had waited until after the funeral.

Jesus, he thought, Benjamin Harrison Jefferson.

XIX

Nudger was standing patiently outside the club, in the red glare of the neon Fat Jack above the sidewalk, when Judy Villanova pushed through the door on her way home from work. It was nine forty-five; she had taken time to change out of her waitress uniform. She was wearing Levi's and a plain white blouse. Despite the red glare, she appeared pale, and even younger than she had inside the club.

Nudger stepped away from the building and moved in front of her, putting on the old sweet smile. "Judy," he said, as if they were longtime friends.

She was on to that approach. As soon as she realized she didn't know Nudger, she stepped nimbly around him and walked fast toward the corner.

Nudger skipped a few steps, then kept pace next to her. "My name is Nudger, Mrs. Villanova. We need to talk. I'm not trying to pick you up; this is business."

She didn't slow down. Didn't so much as glance in his direction. She was a speedy walker for such a small woman; Nudger knew he'd soon be short of breath.

"Please," he said.

The magic word. She dropped back to a pace he could keep up with, looked over at Nudger, studying him, then stopped and stood still near the corner.

"What is it we need to talk about?" she asked.

"Max Reckoner."

She began walking again, but slowly, strolling through the thick, warm evening. Night moths circling the streetlight above cast dappled, flitting shadows over her. Nudger fell into step beside her. She gave him a slow sideways glance. "Why ask me about Max?"

"I was told that you know him."

"I did. I don't anymore."

She began to step down off the curb to cross the street. Nudger stopped her, gripping her gently by the elbow. She was so daintily boned, so breakable. "Look, Judy, I don't want to pry into your private life."

"Then why do it?'

"It's part of my job, but only as far as Max Reckoner is concerned. I'm interested in him, not in you. I'm not even interested in your past relationship with him."

"Just what is your job, Mr. Nudger?"

"You might call me a journalist."

"I might, but I won't. You've been sniffing around Ineida Mann, asking the kind of questions a journalist wouldn't ask."

"Sniffing around?" Nudger said. He didn't like it expressed quite that way; it made him sound like some sort of sex-starved carnivore.

She smiled angelically at him and removed his hand from her elbow. Her pale, slender fingers were surprisingly strong. Possibly she was surprisingly strong in a lot of ways.

And wiser than her youthful appearance suggested. "Level with me, Mr. Nudger," she said.

He walked beside her across Bourbon Street, then west on Royal. "Why don't we go in somewhere, have a cup of coffee, where we can talk without getting winded?"

"I don't want to miss the streetcar and have to stand and wait for another one."

"I'm working for Fat Jack," Nudger said. "If I ask him, he'll instruct you to cooperate with me. But he doesn't know about this conversation and he doesn't have to." Her pace became more deliberate and she glared at him. Oh, he was a bad one, the glare said. He shrugged. "You did say you wanted me to level with you."

She gave him something of a sneer and kept on walking. They were passing some nightspots now, jazz clubs. Music drifted out to them, mingling into a kind of discordant medley that was oddly pleasing to the ear. Nudger thought he picked up a few bars of "Satin Doll." He stayed silent and let Judy Villanova mull things over.

"You don't want to know about me and Max?" she said.

"No."

"Then what do you want to know?"

"About Max and Ineida Mann."

"Know about them how?"

"Man-and-woman stuff. Hanky-panky. Love in the afternoon, or at any hour."

"I don't know for sure, but I don't think there's anything between them. Not that Max wouldn't want there to be."

"How does Ineida feel about Max?"

"She likes him as a friend, but that's all. She's told him that. At first Max thought she was coming on to him, putting on a dumb act and not discouraging him. Then he realized she really is a little slow on the uptake when it comes to the kind of practiced moves he has."

"What was Max's reaction when she told him she wasn't interested in him?"

"A smile and a shrug and a let's-be-friends, and a waiting attitude. It really was nothing to Max. Ineida is just one of many pretty baubles out there for the taking. Like exotic tropical fish in a private lake. He casts his line; if they take the bait, fine. If they don't, that's okay, too. There's always tomorrow."

"You paint him as a shallow, easy-going kind of lothario."

"He is. I know; I'm one of many authorities on Max Reckoner."

"You don't seem the type to get involved with someone like that, Judy."

"Listen, Nudger, Max is a charmer, an expert at exploiting weakness, and I was having trouble with my husband. I was vulnerable; most women are vulnerable at one time or another in their marriage."

"I've heard that theory."

"I'll just bet you have. You married?"

"Divorced."

"Uh-huh."

What did she mean by that? Nudger wondered. None of his business, he decided. Not much about Judy Villanova was any of his business. He said, "Sorry, I promised not to pry into your personal life."

"Gerald—that's my husband—never found out about me and Max. Not many people know about what happened between us. How did you find out?"

"I can't tell you that."

"Why not?"

"I promised someone I wouldn't."

"Maybe you could break that promise."

"No. I'd sooner break the law."

"Old-fashioned man of your word, huh?"

"That's not the kind of thing that's affected by time or fashion."

"No, I guess it isn't." She smiled up at him like the ethereal child she would be until she hit senility. The music trailing them, a sultry jazz number, didn't fit her image.

"What about Sandra Reckoner?" Nudger asked. "What's her attitude toward Ineida?"

"She knows her husband is hot to get into Ineida's unsoiled panties, but that doesn't put Ineida into any special category. My impression is that Sandra puts up with Max's swordsmanship because she has no choice. And she's smart enough not to blame the women Max gets involved with; she knows if it weren't his present lover, it would be another."

"Who's he involved with now?"

"I have no idea." She laughed. "Maybe he's resting; he must sometime."

"Have you heard anything about Sandra Reckoner taking her own lovers while Max is busy?"

Judy lifted her narrow shoulders in an elegant shrug. "I've heard stories about her. So what? If the stories are true, I don't blame her."

"Ever hear of her being involved in kinky sex?" Nudger asked.

"Why, Mr. Nudger, you're beginning to sound like a dirty old man."

Old? Nudger winced. But he knew that to Judy, he was old. So much depended on perspective. It was what made his job difficult.

"But no," Judy said, "I never heard anything like that about her. But then, maybe it's true and I just haven't heard about it."

She turned her head suddenly. They had reached the streetcar stop on St. Charles just in time. With a loud clinking and metallic squeaking of springs, a top-heavy, large box with square windows was swaying around the corner two blocks down.

"I would like for my husband not to know about this conversation, Mr. Nudger. I don't want old coals raked over."

"Gerald won't know. Fat Jack won't know."

"I hope your word really is good in all seasons."

"Oh, it is." The streetcar had stopped for passengers down the block and now was gliding toward them, moving smoothly for such an awkward object. "Is there really one?" Nudger asked.

"One what?"

"A streetcar named Desire."

"There was when Tennessee Williams made it famous. It's a bus route now, Mr. Nudger. Desire is a street." She dug into her white straw purse for change.

"Some street," Nudger said.

"Some street," she agreed.

"I'd appreciate your word that you won't tell Ineida or Willy Hollister about this conversation," Nudger said.

She smiled. "You have it. I won't tell Sandra Reckoner, either."

"Sandra Reckoner?"

"She's the one you really wanted to learn about, not Ineida."

The streetcar swayed to a stop in front of her. It was dirty dark green trimmed in red. The folding front door hissed open.

"Are you a student of psychology at Loyola," Nudger asked, "or do you teach it?"

She nodded good-night to him as she climbed up into the streetcar. He watched through the lighted windows as she paid her fare and found a seat. She didn't look out at him as the streetcar pulled smoothly away and with a faint whine of metal on strained metal continued down St. Charles.

Nudger watched it until it disappeared around a curve, orange sparks flaring from the overhead wire that gave it life.

Desire is a street, all right, he thought.

XX

After talking with the too-perceptive Judy Villanova, Nudger returned to Fat Jack's club for his car, then drove the red subcompact back to the Hotel Majestueux. Some of the streets were rough cobblestone, original New Orleans; he considered clamping a wadded handkerchief in his teeth to keep from losing a filling.

Apparently there was some sort of convention going on at the hotel; several people in identical green blazers were milling about on the sidewalk outside the entrance, and Nudger couldn't find a parking space within two blocks.

He made sure he wasn't in a no-parking zone, locked the car, and started walking back to the hotel. Passing a man and woman who were also wearing green blazers, he saw that they had large plastic nameplates pinned to their lapels that identified them as real estate agents. The women's nameplate read, "Hi, friend, I'M MINDY." She smiled brightly at Nudger, then saw that his jacket was not green but brown, and looked away.

Two paces past her, Nudger stopped and stood still. There was a large man standing alone in the light beneath the hotel's gold canopy. He was staring idly out toward the street as he touched a match to a stubby cigar clamped between his teeth.

Nudger took a few tentative steps closer to make sure of the man's identity.

He hadn't been mistaken; the big man was Dwayne Frick. And probably Frick was waiting for him; there were better places to smoke a cigar than out on the sidewalk surrounded by real estate salespeople in currency-green blazers.

But wasn't real estate a safe investment? Among all those people, he could walk right past Frick without fear of physical harm or another unsettling conversation.

On the other hand, Nudger didn't have to walk past Frick at all. Frick didn't even have to see him. The big man didn't figure to stand out in front of the hotel all evening. Nudger slipped an antacid tablet into his mouth; it might be a good idea to go someplace and get a bland late-night snack to help settle his stomach. Come to think of it, he was even a little hungry.

He turned to walk to his car and bounced back several feet off the massive chest of Rocko Boudreau. Frack.

"Nice that we should bump into each other, eh?" Frack said. He was witty tonight. He wasn't smiling; he had his right hand resting on Nudger's shoulder, ever so gently. But that could change instantly.

Nudger quickly chewed and swallowed his antacid tablet, before Frack did anything that might make him choke on it.

Frack bent slightly to sniff Nudger's minty breath. "Stomach tablets again? You must live on them things. Maybe me and Frick can arrange for you to see a doctor, get some real medicine." Now he smiled his creepy, shadowy smile at Nudger, and his grip on Nudger's shoulder tightened slightly. It felt like the first quarter turn of a vise.

Obviously, Frack wanted Nudger to stay still and not give any sign that he was under duress. Nudger decided it would be easier to obey than not. Where did he have to go, anyway?

"The world is in too much of a hurry, the way I see it," Frack said. "Ain't no point in you adding to all that moving around." The eerie smile again. "World'd be better off if lots of folks just laid themselves down and stayed still forever."

Nudger might have debated that point if fear hadn't welded his tongue to the roof of his mouth. He forgot about Frack's doctor remark; he knew what Frack meant by "still forever."

A black Lincoln sedan pulled to the curb next to them and the driver reached over with a ham-sized hand and opened the passenger side door. Frick must have driven around the block. He glanced up at Nudger before straightening again behind the steering wheel. "Ah, hello, my friend," he said in his syrupy Cajun accent. His diamond-chip gray eyes picked up the dim green light of the dashboard and looked catlike. Nudger felt no warmth from the greeting as Frack shoved a hip into him to guide him into the passenger's seat.

When Nudger was seated, Frack slammed the door, then got in back directly behind Nudger. Nudger wondered if Frack had a gun, then decided it hardly made a difference; that industrial-strength hand was back on his shoulder.

There was a muffled, not-quite-synchronized series of clicks as Frick locked all the Lincoln's doors with the driver's controls, then he shifted his massive bulk beside Nudger to check the rearview mirror, and the car pulled away from the curb. The knots of green-jacketed people, engrossed in trading techniques for steering clients away from faulty furnaces and toward acceptable mortgage financing, gave no sign that anyone had noticed Nudger's skillfully contrived abduction.

"I suppose you wonder where we're taking you," Frick said, making a smooth right turn onto a dark street.

"Not until this very instant," Nudger told him. He was surprised by his flash of what he knew to be temporary bravado. It was obvious that nothing was going to happen to him until they reached their destination. That brief stretch of time looked long and luxurious to a man who thought his life might be at stake. Nudger could feel and appreciate the preciousness of each passing second, almost as if he could reach out and caress time. Einstein knew what he was talking about when he said time was relative and passed faster when you were with your best girl than when you sat down by mistake on a hot stove. That Einstein.

"Your sense of humor will disappear, my friend," Frick said, "when we get where we are going."

Frick knew his stuff as well as Einstein knew his. Even the dark humor of desperation evaporated when time was up against a brick wall. When the Lincoln slowed and turned into a dark alley between a closed office building and a seedy hotel, Nudger's stomach tried to get out of the car and run, growling for him to follow.

But he couldn't move. He was sitting staring through the windshield, paralyzed with the realization of his impending death, memorizing every detail of the alley: the high dim light at the end, faintly illuminating the shadowed, iron-grilled windows; the hulking trash dumpster looming like a military tank halfway down the alley; the stack of damp-ness-distorted cardboard boxes with their plastic-wrapped refuse bursting from separated seams. This was how it would end. They'd find his body here tomorrow. Livingston would hear about it, tell someone that Nudger should have listened to him. Hammersmith would be notified, tell someone that Nudger should have listened to him. Hammersmith would tell Claudia; she would agree that he should have listened. Nudger agreed; he should have listened.

"Can't you hear so good, my friend?" Frick was saying. He'd gotten out of the car and walked around. He was holding the car door open for Nudger. Frack had gotten out of the back and was standing next to Frick, smiling down at Nudger.

That was when Nudger remembered the swamp. Maybe they were going to kill him here, put him in the car's trunk, and drive to where they could hide his body in the bayou. The idea of being under all that muck horrified Nudger; there would be nothing to breathe there, only ooze to suck into his lungs. Then he realized that how and what he breathed would hardly be a problem. He shivered, as if a faint, chill breeze had danced down the alley.

"He don't listen for shit," Frack said. "He pays attention just for a while, and then he has to talk."

"He's not talking now," Frick said.

He started to yank Nudger from the car, but Nudger shoved his big hand away and got out himself and stood in the alley. For the first time since he'd seen Frick standing in front of the hotel, his stomach was calm, his mind strangely placid with resignation. Now he could accept what was about to happen. What, in fact, in all but the heart-ceasing details, *had* happened. But he wouldn't make it easy for them; he owed the old, once-alive Nudger that much.

He backed a quick step, clenched his fist, and threw a straight right hand at Frack's chin, leaning into it to get all his weight behind the blow.

"Jesus," Frack said almost sadly, slipping the punch and pushing Nudger into Frick. Frick drove the tips of his fingers into Nudger's stomach. The wind whooshed out of Nudger as he was spun half around and his hands were pinned behind his back in Frack's relentless grip.

"This one is moderately game," Frick said, amused. He pressed a hand to the side of Nudger's neck and applied pressure. Almost immediately Nudger became dizzy, nauseated. He managed to free one arm and struck blindly at Frick, heard Frick say in his odd courtly manner, "Please, there will be less inconvenience for everyone, my friend, if you cooperate."

For just an instant Nudger felt a pain near the small of his back, so sharp that it took away what ability he'd regained to breathe. Then he was staring up at the lane of black night sky between the tops of the buildings, and the hard paving bricks were pressing into his back.

His left leg was bent under him at a sharp angle; he was sliding hard into third base after his sizzling line drive to left had been booted by Ackie, the Roans' left fielder. Then dynamite exploded behind his right ear; the cut-off man on the Roans had thrown low and hit him in the head with the baseball. He realized what had happened, even as he lost consciousness, even as the Roans' chubby third baseman— Ronny? Rolly?—tried to recover the ball, lost his footing, and fell on top of him.

"Could be a concussion," somebody said. "Hell no, he wasn't safe!" somebody else said. His father was bending over him, large features wavering, speaking as if to someone else. "Little League baseball is rough," he told Nudger.

"Rough," Nudger agreed. His voice was deep, hoarse. Strange. A man's voice. He wasn't lying on the ball diamond in Forest Park in St. Louis. He was miles and years away from there, in an alley in New Orleans.

He tried to sit up and realized that Frick and Frack had treated him more brutally than the Roans' cut-off man. Those guys were sluggers, not shortstops. Pain erupted in Nudger like a nuclear reaction, spreading from his torso down each of his limbs. Bile rose like a solid, bitter column of fire in his throat. He tried to swallow it back down; instead he vomited.

He lay still and tried to regulate his breathing. The pain abated somewhat. Slowly he raised his right hand and wiped his mouth, ran his fingertips over his face. It felt all right. Same familiar features. He used both hands to explore himself and the paving stones on which he lay. No cuts or abrasions. No blood. Nudger knew he'd been the victim of a very professional beating; one that induced pain but no outward evidence of physical violence. Nothing to show the law, to demonstrate with photographs in court. Real pros, were Frick and Frack; all of the damage they'd inflicted was within, like scrambling an egg inside its shell.

The egg rolled over, moaned. Several people strolled past the mouth of the alley, but none of them glanced into its darkness.

It was a full twenty minutes before Nudger managed to get to his feet. He leaned against a brick wall and probed his body for injuries. His ribs seemed okay. There were no mushy spots on his skull. His arms and legs worked, but stiffly and painfully. What the hell had they used on him, rubber hoses?

With an intense effort of will, Nudger made his seemingly disconnected legs propel him jerkily from the alley out onto the sidewalk. It seemed to take several seconds for each signal from his brain to reach his muscles. It was as if he were slow-walking through a nightmare. And maybe he was.

Then he was standing with one foot on the sidewalk, one foot off the curb. He wondered how he could alleviate that problem; it seemed he couldn't move the foot in the street. It was glued down firmly, part of the concrete. Half a dozen people walked past him; they didn't have any idea how to help him, or else they assumed he was drunk. One of them, a woman, even laughed.

"Hey, my man, you sick or something?"

A car was in front of him. For an instant Nudger felt terror. Then he saw the light on top of the car, the lettering on the door.

The police?

He squinted. No, a cab. The driver must have seen him standing half in the street and thought he was hailing a taxi.

"You sick or something?" the cabby repeated.

"Something," Nudger mumbled. He lurched toward the cab and got the rear door open, slumped inside onto the back seat. He hit his head on the roof going in but barely felt it.

"Hospital?" the driver asked, giving him a level, appraising stare in the rearview mirror.

"Hotel Majestueux," Nudger said, letting the cab's soft upholstery envelope him like a mother.

"Hell, that's right around the corner."

"Then drive around awhile before you go there. I need a few minutes."

"You look like you need more than that, mister. I'll get you to a doctor."

"There'll be one at the hotel if I need him."

"You'll need him."

"You forgot to start your meter."

The cabby sighed and pulled the taxi away from the curb. "Left or right?" he asked at the corner as he waited for the light to turn green.

"Either," Nudger said. "It doesn't matter."

"Nope," the cabby said, "I guess it don't."

Nudger managed to walk through the lobby without bending over from the pain in his sides. He'd run up a twenty-dollar taxi fare, but he figured it was worth it; he'd needed the time to recuperate enough to make his way to his room. When he got there, he'd take careful inventory of himself. He really might need a doctor, but he doubted it; Frick and Frack were too good at their job actually to snap or rupture something. Their stock-in-trade was internal bruises, and they were craftsmen.

There was no one else in the elevator, or in the hall, as he made his way to his room. Good. He didn't want to attract attention. The pain was wearing him down, causing him to hunch his shoulders and bend at the waist.

He tried three times before he fumbled the key into the lock. Then he turned the knob, shoved in on the door, and staggered into the room.

It was dark, almost totally; only a tall rectangle of lighter-gray shadow that was the window. He felt around on the wall, found the light switch, and flipped it.

He drew in his breath, making a harsh sound that startled him.

Sandra Reckoner was sitting on the foot of the bed with her long legs crossed, grinning. She was holding a half-full bottle of Southern Comfort and appeared to be a little drunk, but all the way undressed. Her clothes were folded neatly on the blue chair by the desk.

Nudger tried to return her grin, but something in him seemed to shift and he groaned. He watched the smile disappear from Sandra's long, bony face. Alarm rearranged her features. She stood up. Boy, did she stand up!

"Nudger, what's wrong?"

"My timing," he said, and stumbled to the bed and collapsed.

XXI

Willy Hollister's timing was better than Nudger's. While Nudger was floating through varying degrees of pain, Hollister was with Ineida.

"What time is it?" she asked him. She lay huddled against him in his bed, her head resting in the crook of his lean arm. They were comfortably spent and cool, covered only by a light sheet; both of them smelled faintly of perspiration transformed to a musky scent by body heat, the result of their desperate coupling of only a few minutes ago.

"Almost midnight," Hollister told her, squinting to see the luminous hands of his watch through the spray of Ineida's dark hair. He bent his head forward and kissed her lightly on the forehead. He loved her. He was reasonably satisfied that he loved her.

"I need to get home," she said.

"Why? You might as well stay here tonight."

"I'm going in to the club early tomorrow morning to talk to Fat Jack about some new arrangements. Marty's going to pick me up at eight; I don't want to have to get up here at seven and try to get home to wait for him."

"Why so early?" Hollister asked.

"It's the only time Fat Jack has free tomorrow."

Hollister knew that Fat Jack was probably humoring Ineida; new arrangements or not, she still would never bring the crowd to its feet. Polite applause, that was what Ineida would have to learn to feed on. It had never been enough for Hollister, but maybe it would be for her. He smiled faintly in the dimness of the bedroom. But what did it matter? His smile widened, unseen. Should he tell her not to bother with the new arrangements? Not to waste her time?

She sat up suddenly, startling him, the curve of her back smooth and pale in the filtered light, her breasts swaying slightly from her abrupt movement. Hollister saw her fumble with something on the table by the bed. A lighter clicked, illuminating with its bluish flame her unlined face with a cigarette protruding from her compressed lips, her eyes narrowed against the smoke. She seldom smoked, but she had read and heard for a long time about the traditional cigarette after sex, and apparently she wanted to experience it. She often smoked after sex. The bedsprings creaked as Ineida settled back down and rested her head again on Hollister's arm.

"Rather have a joint?" he asked her. "I've got some good Colombian."

"No, I'll just smoke this and then leave."

Hollister rested his head back on the pillow, listening to her long, easy intakes and expulsions of breath as she worked on the cigarette. She was breathing mostly through her nose. He had never seen her actually take smoke into her lungs except for the few times she had smoked marijuana.

Ineida did love him, he was sure. Probably more than he loved her. It would soon be time for the pain, the way it always happened in love. His father had treated him so well after the pain of Willy's mother's death when Willy was only ten years old. The beatings had abruptly ceased. His father's drinking had begun. Then, after the drinking, the eyes-rolled-back, falling-in-the-aisles religion. And his father hadn't let them take Willy away after that incident at school with Iris Crane, take him where they could inject him with drugs and probe his mind with subtle sharp questions.

Had he seen his father's hand dart out and edge his mother from the hayloft door? He couldn't know beyond doubt. His father, surprised to see him standing by the hen-house staring at his mother's limp body, registered nothing but numb disbelief on his rough farmer's face. One second Willy's mother had been standing with him, talking and looking out over the just-seeded fields, the next second she was fifty feet below on the bare ground, dead.

Hollister couldn't be sure of what he'd seen that day. He knew that even his father probably wasn't sure about what had happened. Hollister had expected maybe a deathbed confession twenty years later in the sterile hospital room, but his father had simply looked at him, not unlike the way he'd stared at him seconds after his mother's plunge to death, and then turned to face the empty bed next to his and died quietly.

Hollister still wasn't sure, not about anything, really, except his music. The fools who knew he was great could never imagine the cost of greatness. The price in pain that had to be paid. The trick was never to reach equilibrium, and to let the genuine agony of loss sing between the notes. How could anyone possibly understand the cost of that if they weren't touched by greatness and the need? The need and the way, and the roar of pain tamed to a seductive whisper. Hollister almost laughed out loud at the way so few could see and feel the deeper, wiser blackness against the night. The precious gain in loss.

Beside him a tiny red meteor arced to the ashtray and Ineida stubbed out her cigarette. She sat up again, then twisted her body and leaned low to kiss him on the lips, his face tented softly by her dangling hair.

She asked the eternal question. "Do you love me?" she said, sitting halfway up, still bent over him. "Do you? Even now that you've found out—"

"That doesn't matter to me," Hollister interrupted. "In fact, I admit I'm pleased about it." He ran a fingertip lightly along the soft inside of her thigh and she sucked in breath sharply and her body twitched with pleasure. "I love you more than you might imagine," he whispered.

"Are you sure?"

"As sure as I've ever been of anything."

She kissed him again, then got up and went into the bathroom. The light from the bathroom window spilled outside and illuminated the courtyard. A corner of the garden was visible through the bedroom window.

Hollister lay quietly staring at the symmetrical dark row of rosebushes. The roses would bloom soon, he knew.

XXII

G od, you're pissing blood."

Sandra Reckoner, shy thing that she was, had stayed after helping Nudger into the bathroom. She stood now near the door, nude and unafraid of what the harsh morning light might reveal about her long body. She had no reason to be afraid; the few stretch marks and the slightly pendulous angle of her breasts somehow seemed only to add to her attractiveness by making her real and sensuous in a way no mere centerfold candidate could approach.

"It's from being punched in the kidneys," Nudger told her, leaning with one hand flat against the wall.

"Don't you think you should see a doctor?"

"No." He pushed away from the wall and turned toward the washbasin.

"Why not?"

"Doctors are like mechanics and a number of other people who charge too much for their services. If you go to them, they'll find all sorts of things wrong."

"That's a stupid attitude."

"It probably is at my age; there could really be all sorts of things wrong with me."

"Doesn't it frighten you, seeing blood in your urine"

"Sure. But it scared me worse the first time, after I'd been kicked in the kidneys a few years ago. But I know now it will eventually take care of itself; the people who did this to me knew just how far to go." He washed his hands, splashed cold water over his face.

"You sound as if you admire their professionalism," Sandra said.

"I don't admire it," Nudger told her, "but I'm counting on it instead of my medical insurance." Insurance which, it occurred to him, might have lapsed. Had he paid that last premium? That was something he'd better remember to check on.

"Do you know who beat you up? And why?"

"Yes and yes," Nudger said. "It was two very large primeval types who were underlining a message they'd delivered to me earlier."

"There's such a thing as the police, you know," Sandra said. "Have you called them?"

"No."

"You should. You were assaulted. I understand there's a city ordinance against beating up out-of-towners. And maybe you could use police protection."

"I'm not so sure, in this instance."

Sandra looked at him curiously. "You weren't in any shape to talk about it last night," she said. "Would it help you to talk about it now?"

"No," Nudger told her, "I don't even want to think about it."

She knew when not to pursue a subject. She stepped around him, bent over and turned on the taps in the bathtub, then pulled the chrome lever that got the shower going. "Wait for the water to get warm," she said. "I'll be right back." She sidestepped around his listing form again and left the bathroom.

Nudger stood remembering his night with her. She had comforted him, held his head close between her bare breasts, as he drifted in and out of sleep, in and out of pain. Several times she had suggested calling the hotel doctor; each time Nudge had refused. In the coolness of the air-conditioned room, it was the heat of her long body that he wanted, the warmth of her limitless compassion. Sex, of course, had been out of the question; Nudger was having enough difficulty simply breathing. But she had stayed with him and given him what at that moment he so badly needed.

Nudger smiled briefly. He had kept his pledge of fidelity to Claudia. He felt rather smug about that.

Sandra returned to the bathroom, wearing her panties and bra. She reached in behind the plastic shower curtain to test the temperature of the hissing water.

"Are you ready for this?" she asked.

Nudger nodded.

She helped him step over the edge of the bathtub; he looked down as he did this and saw that his body showed only a few faintly purple bruises and was almost unmarked by one of the worst beatings he'd ever endured.

"Can you stand up by yourself all right in there?" Sandra asked over the rush of water.

"I can stand and move around okay," Nudger told her. "It just hurts when I do." The needles of hot water seemed to penetrate his flesh and soothe his stiffened and abused muscles. He looked over at Sandra, smiled at the concern on her bony features. "I'm on the mend," he assured her.

She nodded, looking no less concerned. "Sure," she said, and pulled the shower curtain closed. He didn't hear her leave, but registered the sharp click of the latch as she shut the bathroom door.

Nudger turned his body slowly to let the water work on his back, then turned again and raised his face into the powerful spray. He stood that way for several minutes, lost in the cascade of hot water. Finally he moved back a step so the spray struck his chest. Steam began to rise. He really could feel his body loosening up, his strength returning.

He stayed in the shower a long time, running up the Hotel Majestueux's water bill. Then he gingerly toweled dry, used his fingers to brush his hair back, and wiped away condensation on the fogged mirror so he could look at himself.

Same old Nudger, but maybe a few years older than he'd been last night.

He walked stiffly out of the bathroom to locate some clothes. Each step made him ache, but less than he'd anticipated, and the pain at the base of his spine was almost gone.

He felt like lying back down, but he knew that if he did his body would stiffen up again and he'd undo much of the good of the hot shower. With the slow deliberation of a man in a dream, he began getting dressed.

Twisting back his arms to get his shirt on was painful, as was crouching braced against the wall to step into his pants. But the shoes and socks were the worst. Bending his body to reach his feet was a rare agony. He managed to get one shoe tied in a bow, then fastened the other one with a crude knot, sat up straight, and said the hell with it.

The effort of getting dressed took more out of him than

he'd thought it would. It also made him realize he was hungry. Should he phone down for a motorized wheelchair with chrome hubcaps, or just call Room Service?

He decided on Room Service and ordered a two-egg cheese omelet, toast, orange juice, and a pot of coffee. Then he unlocked the door, slumped in the blue armchair, and for the first time looked at his wristwatch. He was surprised to see that it was almost eleven o'clock. Sandra Reckoner had given him her morning as well as her night, without much in return.

Nudger realized that either the maid was late this morning or she'd found his door locked with the nightlatch and would make up his room on her late rounds. It occurred to him that she might come in at the same time as the bellhop from Room Service and bustle over to the wastebasket and empty it. That could cause minor complications; Nudger decided he'd better remove the stack of Ineida's love letters from the wastebasket where they were concealed inside the wadded napkin.

He stood up and creaked over to the desk, placing his left palm on it to support himself while he leaned over the wastebasket and felt beneath crumpled papers to find the napkin.

As soon as he touched the napkin he knew something was wrong; it was lying flat, not the way he'd carefully arranged it to conceal the letters.

Blood was rushing to his head, making him dizzy, so he straightened, lifting the metal waste-basket as he did so and setting it on the desk. He stuck his hand in the wastebasket and probed around; still no letters. To be sure, he dumped the contents onto the desk.

The letters were gone.

"Damn her!" he said softly, but with enough vehemence to make his sides ache from the effort of abruptly expelled air.

At the knock on the door, he scooped the trash back into the wastebasket and set it on the floor. Then he hobbled over to the door and opened it, expecting to say hello to his breakfast.

But it wasn't Room Service at the door.

It was Ineida Mann.

XXIII

Not Ineida Collins, Ineida Mann. She'd shed her
ingenue image for her visit with Nudger. She was
wearing tight black leather slacks that laced up the
fly, and a navy-blue blouse with an oversized collar. Her
dark high heels made her seem six inches taller than the little girl who sang. She had on a spiked gold bracelet clasped
tight around her wrist, and she was clutching a small leather
purse in such a way that the long, thin strap dangled from
her hand like a whip. Nudger thought she looked as if she'd
been hanging around someplace taming lions.

"I want to talk to you," she said, pitching her voice low,
biting off the words hard. Everything about her was hard
today except for her eyes. They tried, but had marshmallow
centers.

Nudger stepped back and motioned for her to come in.
She stalked into the room, then paused, noticing that he was
walking with difficulty.

"What's wrong with your legs?" she asked.

"I had an accident. Sliding into third base."

She looked at him strangely but didn't press with more questions. That she wasn't here about the letters was obvious; she wasn't clawing at Nudger or threatening a lawsuit. Or maybe she was working up to that. Actually she would approach him differently, Nudger knew, if she found out that he'd stolen and read her sometimes clinical love missives to Willy Hollister; he would hear from her not at all, or he would hear from her attorneys.

Standing just inside the door, she spread her feet wide and faced him squarely, establishing a beachhead that she might just expand into a full-scale invasion. "Why are you investigating me?" she asked.

"I'm not," Nudger told her, which seemed for this occasion close enough to the truth.

Her greenish eyes narrowed and managed to become tigerish. She'd practiced the expression; she was doing it consciously to demonstrate her anger. Nudger figured she was actually scared beneath all that bravado and makeup. "You're asking questions about me," she said. "Coming around my apartment lying to me, sneaking around the club. Does my father have something to do with this?"

"Not exactly."

"Do you know who he is?"

"Yes." Nudger was getting tired of standing. He made his way painfully over to the blue armchair and eased back down into it. The old chair felt pretty good.

Ineida placed her fists on her hips and jutted out her smooth fighting chin. Nudger thought she might have a brighter future as an actress than as a singer. "If my father didn't hire you to spy on me, who did?"

"I'm not spying on you, Ineida. And you enter into my job only in a way that could prove beneficial to you."

"That's vague, Nudger. I didn't come here to listen to you be vague."

"Sorry. I feel vague this morning."

Standing in such a dramatic spread-legged fashion in those high heels must have gotten to her ankles. She stood up straighter and more naturally, her feet closer together so her weight bore down evenly and more comfortably on the thin spike heels.

"Why are you dressed that way?" Nudger asked.

"Dressed what way?"

"Like a dominatrix in a cheap whorehouse."

She blinked at him; she didn't know what he meant. Women who whipped masochistic men for pay were beyond her experience and imagination. Her ignorance was inexcusable, she figured, so without answering she reached into her purse and tossed a fat white envelope into Nudger's lap.

"What's this?" Nudger asked, leaving the envelope alone. But he knew what it was, just not how much.

She told him. "Twenty thousand dollars."

He was impressed, and not nearly so altruistic and unswerving. Then, when he saw Ineida smile at him, he picked up the envelope and tossed it back to her. To his surprise, she caught it left handed with the ease of a major league first baseman and stood holding it.

The smile stayed, a confident curve above the arrogant chin. "You don't believe me," she said. "Would you like to see the money? Count it?"

"No," he told her, "seeing all that money might break down my resolve. I'm not made of wood; mostly I'm papier-mâché made from unpaid bills."

"Then accept this." She extended the envelope toward him but didn't toss it this time. "Go back to where you came from and forget this job. But first, tell me who hired you. And why."

"I can't do that, Ineida. Ethics." He thought about her love letters he'd stolen, now missing from his possession, and his stomach twitched.

She saw that he was serious, then stopped smiling and replaced the bulging envelope in her purse. Nudger watched its fat white form disappear; absently he wiped his hand across his mouth. "You really do have ethics," she said, almost in amazement.

"Sure. You find them in unexpected places," he told her, "like lost buttons." Probably she hadn't seen much in the way of ethics, being David Collins' daughter. "Have you talked to your father about this?"

"No. What good would it do? If he did hire you, or knew who did, he'd just lie to me about it. He considers me too young to know certain things, still a child."

"Where did you get the twenty thousand dollars?" Nudger asked.

"It's mine; I have money of my own." She gazed curiously at Nudger. "Are you working for my father and afraid to accept the money?"

"No."

"If that's the situation, twenty thousand dollars can take you a long way from New Orleans."

"Not that I'm working for him," Nudger said, "but if we got into a contest to see who could afford the most one-way tickets, he'd win."

She knew Old Dad well enough not to argue with Nudger on that point. "I don't like being watched over as if I'm a twelve-year-old," she said.

"Most people don't. Especially twelve-year-olds. Does Willy Hollister know you came here?"

The chin was out again. "Of course not! He doesn't know my family has money. No one in the jazz scene knows it, or knows my true identity."

"They won't learn who you are from me," Nudger told her.

"How did you find out who I am, if Daddy didn't tell you?"

"I learned from someone else. You're from New Orleans, Ineida; how long do you think you can sing in a club without someone recognizing you?"

"I've spent the last six years away from the city, and the kind of people in my old circles don't go to jazz clubs off Bourbon Street." She smiled again with that unassailable blind confidence. "And I don't look at all the way I used to, Nudger; I've grown up."

"In some very obvious ways," Nudger said, letting his gaze flick up and down her tightly clad body. She liked that, he could tell. Would she try to bribe him with something other than money?

"Now," she said, lowering her head and fixing him with an upcast, direct stare, still smiling.

"Now what?" Nudger asked, wondering if a lot of people had been wrong about Ineida.

But the thought of tit for tat, sex for that, hadn't entered her naive young mind. Or if it had; it had fled through the pure driven snow. "Now are you going to tell me who hired you if Daddy didn't?"

"Nope," Nudger said, wondering if he was disappointed.

There was a polite knock on the door. Ineida looked in that direction, then back at Nudger, and he nodded, motioning for her to answer the knock. "That would be Room Service."

Ineida went to the door, opened it, and stood back.

A scrawny young bellhop Nudger hadn't seen before pushed a cart with Nudger's breakfast on it into the room. When he saw Ineida in her *Hustler* magazine outfit, his Adam's apple jumped but his expression remained professionally bland. The cart's wheels squeaked as he ran it through a kind of loose figure eight.

"For him," Ineida said, pointing toward Nudger.

The kid gulped noisily and pushed the cart over to the blue chair. Nudger nodded thanks to him and tried to reach into his hip pocket for his wallet without standing up. He found that the pocket was empty, and he saw his wallet on the dresser where Sandra Reckoner had put it after it had fallen onto the floor while she was helping him to undress last night.

"Here," Ineida said, holding out a five-dollar bill for the scrawny kid. He accepted the money and grinned at her; he liked her, all right. Nudger wished he'd take her out for a PG movie and a hamburger and a Coke and make her forget all about Willy Hollister.

When the bellhop had gone, she turned again to Nudger, who was meticulously placing a napkin in his lap and lifting the silver cover off his plate. Eggs, toast, and coffee had never smelled so good.

"Your last chance," she said, tilting her halfopen purse so he could see a corner of the white envelope. With the sight seemed to come the faint perfumed scent of money to mingle with his breakfast aromas.

Nudger ignored her, tried not to look at the envelope.

"Aren't you even tempted?"

"Of course I am."

"Then why don't you accept my offer?"

"You said it earlier: scruples."

"I said ethics."

"Same thing."

"Same price, too. I don't think you're not for sale, Nudger; I think it's simply that someone is paying you more than my offer. How much more?"

"Don't be ridiculous. No one has more money than you do."

Nudger's refusal was puzzling and infuriated her. This visit wasn't going as she'd anticipated. She hadn't planned on a smitten bellhop and a private investigator dumb enough to have more of an appetite for food than for money. Life was too damned tricky and unpredictable. Unfair, unfair. Something inside her began to cave in. She suddenly looked even more ridiculous in the MTV clothes she'd worn to impress him with her authority. Different dress and mannerisms hadn't taken her where she wanted to go.

"I want you to leave me alone," she said, almost crying because she couldn't buy what she wanted. "I want you to stop sneaking around and badgering me and Willy and threatening our happiness."

"You have a few things backward," Nudger told her.

"No, I don't. And I get what I want, Nudger." Her eyes were brimming; she looked so young and unknowing, standing there on the edge of tears and rage, ready to topple forward on those high heels and fall in. So very, very determined. "I'll get you to leave Willy and me alone, no matter what it takes."

"A threat?"

"A threat," she confirmed. She was trembling, about to lose any semblance of control over her emotions.

"Do you want half of my omelet?" Nudger asked her.

"No! Do me a favor and choke on your goddamned omelet!"

Unwilling to break down in front of him, she stalked

from the room quickly so he couldn't see the sobbing that he heard. She slammed the door so hard that the omelet quivered on its plate like something alive and neurotic.

Nudger sat in the reverberating silence for a few minutes, then pushed his plate away and poured himself a cup of coffee. Ineida and her tears and her twenty thousand dollars had ruined his appetite.

After coffee and half a piece of buttered toast, Nudger went to the bed and sat down with the phone. He dialed direct to the Third District station house in St. Louis and got Hammersmith.

"This is Nudger, Jack."

"I know," Hammersmith said, "I was warned."

Nudger made a mental note not to leave his name next time with Ellis the desk sergeant. "I need some information."

"I assume you're still in New Orleans, or you'd be here in the flesh to bring to bear the full force of your personality behind your request. What specifically do you want to know?"

"Nothing specifically," Nudger said. "I want your feeling on the Billy Weep murder."

"You mean Benjamin Harrison Jefferson?"

"You know who I mean," Nudger said.

"My feeling, huh?" Hammersmith understood what Nudger was requesting.

Nudger heard the labored wheezing sounds of Hammersmith lighting a cigar and was glad that over six hundred miles separated them. Even at that he considered glancing out the window to check wind direction.

"We found a gram of heroin hidden in Weep's apartment, Nudge," Hammersmith said.

"I thought you searched his apartment and came up with nothing."

"This was wrapped in a cut-off prophylactic and tucked down into a light socket with a bulb screwed in on top of it. Would you have found it?"

"No," Nudger said, letting Hammersmith extract his price for whatever information he was going to divulge, making a resolution not to take burned-out light bulbs for granted. They and burned-out people could surprise.

"The most likely theory is that someone knew Weep had the junk hidden in the apartment and killed him for it but didn't find it." Hammersmith couldn't quite make himself sound as if he believed that theory.

"How would they know he had it or how much it was?"

"Could be they saw him get it from his supplier and followed him home."

Nudger remembered the wasted Billy Weep slouched in his chair in the shadows. It was hard to imagine him having the strength even to go out and score for a fix. And it wasn't easy to find a supplier who delivered heroin like pizza to go. Something softer, maybe, but not heroin. "Was there evidence of heroin in his blood?" Nudger asked.

"No. There was a two-point-five alcohol reading and there were traces of THC in him. Marijuana. He was on two kinds of high when he was killed."

"Maybe not," Nudger said. "THC stays around in the body for a long time, and when I talked to him just before his death, Billy told me he wasn't drinking."

"That may or may not be true about the drinking, Nudge. The ME says his liver was about gone and he'd have probably died within six months on his own if somebody hadn't helped him across."

"How about needle tracks?" Nudger asked. "Did the ME find any on Billy's body?"

Hammersmith smacked his lips and puffed on his cigar;

over the phone he sounded like a locomotive in heat. "How astute of you to ask, Nudge. No needle-entry signs, not under the tongue or between the toes or anywhere else."

"Do you know what was used to beat him to death?"

"No. It could have been a number of things. He actually died of asphyxiation."

"Asphyxiation?" Nudger repeated. "Somebody choked him?"

"Whatever was used on him hit him in the throat, crushed his larynx and windpipe cartilage, made it impossible for him to get air."

Nudger couldn't help it; he imagined for a moment how it would be, the final, horrible panic: thrashing around wildly on the floor, struggling futilely to suck in oxygen, feeling your heart sledgehammer against your ribs, your entire body about to crumple inward around its internal airless ruins. The rage. The terror.

Hammersmith surprised Nudger. "I'm sorry, Nudge. Was he a pretty good friend?"

"To a lot of music lovers," Nudger said. "You haven't answered my question, Jack."

"I know. I'm not sure how I feel about this one. Could be the obvious—old junkie followed home and killed for his stash."

"Or it could be that somebody planted the heroin to make it look that way."

"A guy that clever," Hammersmith said, "he's smart enough to buy a plane ticket south. All the way to New Orleans." Slurp, wheeze on the cigar. "You see any connection down there with Weep's death?"

"Nothing firm. Hollister maybe, but I checked him out. He didn't have a chance to leave town and get back here the night Billy was murdered. The times don't quite fit."

"My clothes don't quite fit, either," Hammersmith said, "but I wear them." Which was a lie; the obese Hammersmith had most of his clothes tailored to his sleek bulk. "Maybe Hollister found a way."

"That would be like a thirty-eight short on you," Nudger said.

Hammersmith said something that sounded like a growl.

"I'll let you know if anything down here does gel," Nudger told him.

"Do that," Hammersmith said. He made another disgusting airy slurping sound with the cigar. "In the meantime, I'll be here standing tall between the citizens and the savages."

"How do you know who's who?" Nudger asked, but a dial tone hit him in the ear. Hammersmith, who had a thing about getting in the last word on the phone, had hung up.

That was okay. He couldn't have answered Nudger's question anyway. Nobody could. That was the world's and Nudger's problem.

XXIV

Who's he working for?" Hollister asked. "I don't know. He won't say." Ineida didn't tell Hollister that she'd offered Nudger money to pull away from whatever his business was in New Orleans. Whatever his interest was in her and Willy.

They were in the Croissant Bar in the French Quarter, where they often shared breakfast in a back booth. Neither was eating today. A blueberry croissant with one small bite out of it lay growing stale on a napkin next to Hollister's steaming coffee cup. There was nothing but an untouched glass of orange juice on the table in front of Ineida. She wasn't feeling well this morning.

"It doesn't matter who he is or who he's working for," Ineida said. "We're not doing anything illegal; he can't do anything about us or to us. We can ignore him." She sounded as if she were trying to convince herself more than Hollister.

After a lot of thought, Hollister had decided on this one last attempt to learn more about Nudger. He wasn't surprised Ineida had failed to do so. But she was right;

they weren't breaking any laws. No one could be arrested for what they were thinking, or for the pain to be.

Long after his mother's death, he had learned to play the blues, the music of the lost. The very core of suffering. He'd learned to draw on the emptiness brought about by his mother dying and the years that followed. He had thought a lot about pain. In school in Illinois. Later in New York. His mother had loved him, and his father had told him after her death how much she had been loved by both of them. Had told him over and over again. Willy had sensed the fear in his father, and the agony. He'd played his father's pain and it had worked; it had permeated his music in the little New York clubs he'd played, then in the blues cities of the Midwest. And when his father died, Hollister found that he could no longer draw on that pain. It didn't matter, he discovered. His own pain worked even better. So much better. But he needed a fix now and then to sustain him. Like a masochist, though he knew he wasn't that; just the opposite. Like a vampire. Just like a vampire. Hollister shuddered. He didn't like the comparison.

"You look tired," Ineida was telling him. "You okay, babe?"

"Didn't sleep much last night," he said. He smiled at her. "I'm not sure why. Thinking of you, maybe. Wishing you were with me even while my mind was working on every other thing that drifted into it."

She touched his hand, returned the smile. She really was a beautiful woman, he thought. He was lucky. The need rose powerfully in him, the terrible need and the regret. Looking into her unknowing eyes, he was pulled in every direction, while something small but wise seemed to walk around the inside of his skull, understanding what it was all about, stage-directing his thoughts and longings.

"Nothing matters to us but us," Ineida said fiercely to him.

Which was almost true, Hollister realized. Almost. He could, if he chose, spend the rest of his life with this woman. He did love her. He looked into her eyes again and told her so.

He could hear the music, now, beckoning him, urging him. But it would be slightly different this time. It would be better.

He closed his eyes for a moment, listening inside himself.

It was time, he knew. In music, timing was everything.

XXV

Nudger thought he'd feel stronger after breakfast. Instead he was slightly nauseated and weaker. Maybe his conversation with Hammersmith had done that to him; maybe the cigar had worked psychologically, even over the phone and all that distance.

When he stood up, a wave of dizziness almost forced him to sit back down. He managed to push the cart with the breakfast dishes outside into the hall, hang the "Do Not Disturb" sign on the doorknob, then lock himself in his room and walk to the bed.

Tired. He hadn't realized how tired he was. Everything that had happened recently seemed to be catching up, enveloping him now. Or was he seeking escape into sleep? Escape from this entire mad business. There were plenty of maybes that might apply. Nudger couldn't figure out exactly why he was suddenly exhausted, but he was; that he knew for sure. He half fell onto the bed and lay on his stomach.

He slept until early evening, then got up in the quiet dusk and staggered into the bathroom to switch on the light and lean over the toilet bowl. He noted with satisfaction that his urine wasn't quite so red. Gee, how could a guy see that and not feel that everything was right with the world?

Nudger knew how, even given as he was to baseless optimism. The pain was back, threatening to get really vicious, so he went back to the bed and lay down, went immediately to sleep again, and slept until nine-twenty the next morning. Time sure flew when you weren't having fun.

Déjà vu seemed to play a prominent role in Nudger's life, he reflected, wondering if it was like that with everyone. This morning was a repeat of yesterday morning, only without Sandra Reckoner. The hot needle shower to ease aches and stiffness, the clean, unwrinkled clothes, the eggs, juice, and coffee served up by the gawky young bellhop who rolled the car in and looked around for Ineida, his protruding Adam's apple bobbing frantically like some kind of carnal radar.

"She's not here," Nudger said.

"Yes, sir," the bellhop answered, leaving the tray in front of the blue chair again. "I can see that." It was as if Nudger had diabolically dictated that Ineida disappear. The kid seemed to hold it against him, so Nudger tipped him a mere dollar and watched him sulk and disappear himself.

Plenty of appetite this morning, and nothing to spoil it. Nudger forked down the omelet, ate every crumb of the toast, and drained his orange juice glass. Then he sat and leisurely sipped two cups of coffee, realizing with hope and satisfaction that he felt tolerably well today. Some pain was still present, but he could tune it out enough to coexist with it. He could be Nudger again, and not merely a thing that lay motionless and ached.

Still moving stiffly, but not nearly as slowly as his creeping pace of yesterday, he gingerly labored into his sport jacket and straightened his open shirt collar. Then he left the hotel and walked through golden-molasses sunshine to Fat Jack's club.

Fat Jack was in his office this morning, at his desk studying a folder full of sheet music with a sketchy and faded look to the notes. He had his suit coat off and was wearing a pristine white shirt with the sleeves rolled up to reveal forearms like fleshy hams.

"Hey, high tech," Fat Jack said. He gave a little off-hand wave.

"Hi," Nudger said, somewhat confused. Had Fat Jack said "tech," or had he greeted him as "Tex"?

"Guy set me some blues numbers written by his computer," Fat Jack explained. Tech. "Wants me to have the band play them some night. Trouble is, the computer doesn't writ e like W. C. Handy, it writes like IBM. Can you believe it, one of the numbers here is called 'Dot Matrix Momma of Mine.' "

"Catchy."

"So's syphilis."

Nudger guessed Fat Jack didn't like the dot matrix number.

"Where you been?" Fat Jack asked.

"Slept late; I was beat."

"Not this morning. I mean yesterday."

"Yesterday morning's when Ineida came to my hotel to see me," Nudger said, turning away the thrust of Fat Jack's question like a seasoned politician on "Meet the Press." "She offered me twenty thousand dollars to leave her and Hollister alone."

Fat Jack looked thoughtful and shifted his immense weight; the chair somewhere beneath him groaned for mercy.

"She said it was her money," Nudger said. "Do you think she could come up with that much on her own without her father knowing about it?"

"He might not know about it now," Fat Jack said, "but you can bet he will know about it, whether it's her money or his." He suddenly glanced sharply up at Nudger. "Hey, how come you turned down her offer?"

Nudger shrugged. "I'll make it up when I send you your bill."

Fat Jack was too lost in concern even to respond to that outrageous suggestion. He used his sausage-fingered left hand to worry the gold pinky ring on his right. "What did she say when you refused her offer, old sleuth?"

"She couldn't understand why she couldn't buy something she wanted that badly. She got mad."

"People like that," Fat Jack said, "they know the value of money. Hey, I mean the real value. Even at her age, been rich all her life. Folks like you and me, we think we understand, but we don't. Usually not till it's too late. You must have confused her for sure, a private cop without a price tag."

"She assumed somebody was paying me more for staying on the job than she was offering me to quit."

"Hey."

"She wants to know what's going on," Nudger said, "wants to know how she figures into it. I think maybe it's time we tell her, see how it all falls."

"No," Fat Jack said quickly. "No matter how it falls, it will all land on me."

"But think how much heavier it will be if David Collins finds out you had information that might have saved his daughter from Hollister and you kept silent."

Fat Jack was scooting one of the computer-composed numbers back and forth on the flat desktop with his fingertips, pondering Nudger's question. Nudger could read the piece's title, even though from his perspective it was upside down: "Floppy Disk Fanny." He liked that one. The desk phone rang.

Fat Jack picked up the receiver, pressed it above the jowl on the right side of his broad head, and identified himself. A few seconds passed, and his face went as white as his shirt.

"Yes, sir" he said. Both jowls began to quiver; loose flesh beneath his left eye started to dance. It was as if the thin man who's supposed to be inside every fat man was struggling to get out. Nudger was getting nervous just looking at him.

"You can't mean it," Fat Jack said. "Hey, maybe it's a joke, is all." Pause. "Okay, it ain't a joke." He listened a while longer and then said, "Yes, sir" again and hung up. He didn't say anything else for a long time. Nudger didn't say anything either. The air conditioner behind the desk hummed and gurgled; traffic outside on Conti swished by with the low, tense singing of rubber on hot pavement.

Fat Jack spoke first. He sounded out of breath. "That was David Collins. Ineida's gone. Not home. Not anywhere. Bed hasn't been slept in."

"Then she and Hollister left as they planned."

"You mean as Hollister planned. Collins got a note in the mail."

"Note?" Nudger asked. His stomach did a flip; it was way ahead of his brain, reacting to a suspicion not yet fully formed.

"A ransom note," Fat Jack confirmed. "Unsigned, in cut-out newspaper words, just like in some cornball TV cop show." Fat Jack paused, perspiring. "Oh, Christ—cop! Collins said Livingston is on his way over here now to talk to me about Hollister."

"Why isn't he on his way to talk to Hollister? That would make more sense."

"No, it wouldn't. Hollister's disappeared, too. And his clothes are missing from his closet." Fat Jack's little pink eyes were bulging in his blanched face. He was suffering plenty; things he couldn't fathom were happening too fast. "We kept quiet too long about them letters you found. I better not tell Livingston about them."

"Not unless he asks," Nudger said. "And he won't."

"If he finds out about them and demands to have them, we're caught between having to withhold evidence or admitting something Collins won't be able to forgive. Some choice!"

"It's not one we'll have to make," Nudger said, "because the letters are gone."

"Huh? Gone where?"

"I don't know. They were stolen from my room."

A tremor ran through Fat Jack with this new source of worry. Its epicenter must have been his heart; he clutched his chest in a way that had Nudger concerned for a moment, then he seemed to calm down and dropped his hands to the desk. "Do you figure Collins might have got them?"

"I think we can rule it out," Nudger said. He knew that if Frick or Frack had been in his room and found the letters, they would have mentioned it to him during their encounter in the alley. Or they would have phoned David Collins for instructions and that encounter would have been far more serious.

"You got any idea who might have the letters?" Fat Jack asked.

"No," Nudger lied. "Have the police been officially contacted about Ineida's kidnapping?"

"Collins isn't the sort to trust the police on something

like this," Fat Jack said. "He'll try taking care of it on his own, and in his own fashion."

Nudger thought about asking how Livingston knew about Ineida's disappearance, but he decided that would be naive.

Fat Jack suddenly grimaced, as if something inside his head had been reeled painfully tight. "Just what the hell am I going to say to Livingston?"

"Play it by ear," Nudger told him. "You've been doing that all your life and it's worked out fine." He stood up.

"Where you going?"

"I'm leaving," Nudger said, "before Livingston gets here. There's no sense in making this easy for him."

"Or difficult for you."

"It works out that way, for a change."

Fat Jack nodded, his eyes unfocused yet thoughtful, already rehearsing in his mind the lines he would use on Livingston. His survival instincts had been aroused. He wasn't a man to bow easily or gracefully to trouble, and he had seen plenty of trouble in his life. He knew a multitude of moves and would use them all.

"By the way," Nudger said, "do you know a woman named Marilyn Eeker?"

"Eeker? . . ." Fat Jack mumbled absently, his mind not on the question. "No, never heard of her."

"A petite blonde, about forty."

Still engrossed in his own worsening dilemma, Fat Jack didn't bother to answer. Maybe he hadn't heard.

He didn't seem to notice when Nudger left.

XXVI

They were waiting for Nudger by his car, around the corner from Fat Jack's. Frick and Frack. His stomach growled something that sounded like "Please, noooo!" He considered turning and running, even though they'd seen him and could easily overtake him. Fear and memory churned around in his gut like something alive and violent. He tried to fight it down; it wouldn't stay.

Nudger figured the best way to deal with this was to walk on to his car and try to hide his fright. His aches from his previous beating seemed to flare up now that he was in the proximity of perpetrators Frick and Frack. He wished he'd stayed in Fat Jack's office and opted for Livingston instead of being here now, walking like a school kid toward two class bullies.

At first Nudger thought the little red subcompact had a flat tire. Then he saw that its left front side was six inches lower than the right because Frick had one of his gigantic feet resting on the bumper. When Nudger got closer the car bobbed level as Frick removed the foot, straightened up, and both men stood facing him squarely, not smiling, waiting for him.

"Don't worry, my friend," Frick told him. "None of the rough persuasion this time."

"Nice of you to let my internal bruises heal," Nudger said, stopping a safe five feet from the two men. His voice hadn't squeaked as much as he'd feared. Traffic continued to flow past where the car was parked; a few drivers slowed down to gawk at the impressive bulk of Frick and Frack, then drove on in a hurry, hoping they hadn't offended with their slackened speed and curious glances, praying their engines wouldn't stall.

"Ain't you gonna have one of those little white things you chew?" Frack asked. He shifted his body to the side and dropped his shoulder slightly, as if ready to throw a stiff left jab, trying to appear more menacing. He didn't need the theatrics; he'd probably menaced his mother's obstetrician upon emergence from the womb.

Nudger obliged him by thumbing an antacid tablet directly from the roll into his mouth. "What's this about?" he asked, chomping loudly, as if noise might bluff away his uneasiness.

"Mr. Collins said you and he need to talk," Frick said.

"About what?"

Frick did smile now. "What difference does it make? Mr. Collins wants a word, my friend, and you can find out what that word is about when he decides to tell you. That's the way it is with Mr. Collins."

"Who am I to break tradition?" Nudger said. He wouldn't push things. He couldn't be sure if Frick and Frack knew about Ineida's disappearance. He would bet that they did, and they were here for that reason. But it seemed unwise to try to anticipate David Collins, so Nudger stayed silent.

"Get in the car," Frack instructed.

Nudger glanced around. "What car? Where is it parked?"

"We're going in your car," Frick said. "That way you won't have to take a cab back to your hotel. You drive."

Nudger didn't argue with such uncompromising consideration. They watched as he unlocked the car. Frick sat in front next to him, knees cranked up almost beneath his chin. Frack was somehow packed into the back-seat area, his huge knees digging into Nudger's back through the thin upholstery of the tiny bucket seat.

"Don't them seats go up farther so I got more room?" Frack asked.

Frick reached down awkwardly, yanked a lever. Instead of moving forward, his seatback slammed backward as far as it would go into the reclining position. It could only go halfway because it hit Frack, who grunted in surprise and pain and shoved the seatback forward again violently, almost causing Frick to strike his head on the windshield.

"Christ!" Frick said. "Easy."

"You guys are too big for this car," Nudger told them, when the subcompact had stopped rocking.

"Fuck it," Frack said. "Drive. We'll give you directions."

Nudger drove.

Less than an hour later, the dwarf auto labored up the long driveway of a plush and rambling Spanish-style house several miles outside the city. It was all stucco and rough-sawn timber, painted white with dark-stained trim. Each end of the wide house was marked by a chopped-off kind of guard tower with small rectangular windows. Just the place for Rapunzel if she were twins. Flowering bougainvillea had crawled halfway up one of the towers and bloomed a wild riot of color, floral anarchists trying to escape from the neatly manicured green shrubbery around the foundation. There was a circular driveway that ran beneath a tile-roofed portico before tall, dark-stained wood front doors adorned with black iron. Beyond the house, where the ground sloped up gradually toward a distant chain-link fence, a gardener was working slowly but diligently with a shovel, piling earth off to the side in a neat mound. Nudger tried not to think of what he might be digging.

The red subcompact strained and clattered up to the crest of the driveway. The overheated little radiator sighed in relief as Nudger obeyed Frick's instructions and parked beneath the portico and finally switched off the engine.

Nudger felt like part of one of those circus acts where a dozen or so clowns pile out of a tiny parked car. What Frick and Frack lacked in numbers, they more than made up for in poundage.

Frick and Nudger stood waiting patiently outside while Frack grunted and growled and levered his contorted body loose from the back of the car. Nudger wondered how he could explain to the rental company how the car had gotten stretched. Did the insurance form he'd signed cover that? As if angry at the car for being small, Frack slammed the door so hard the window almost popped out.

With Nudger between them, the two big men stepped up on the porch, pushed open the doors without knocking, and entered the house; they were familiar with their imposing surroundings, and they had returned with what they'd been sent to get.

The interior of the house was as plush as the exterior suggested it would be. There were acres of tiled floor, expensive-looking throw rugs, heavy Spanish-style furniture, ornately framed oils hung on the sand-finished walls. Nothing seemed to be used or worn in the slightest; it was as if professional decorators had placed the furnishings just so and then left things to be dusted lightly by someone every few days.

Frick led the way down a hall, through a door, and down a flight of wide, brightly lighted stairs. Another door opened into what Nudger assumed was the house's basement level. He was beginning not to like this.

They walked down another hall, this one lined with more paintings. These were unlike the traditional oils upstairs; they were modern, canvases splashed with indecipherable forms that were somehow ominous. Jackson Pollock possessed by Poe.

Frick stopped near a bend of the hall, stepped to the side, and motioned for Nudger to turn the corner first.

Nudger did, not without apprehension, and there was a small, dark-haired man sitting in one of half a dozen black leather chairs in a large, carpeted room.

Unlike upstairs, this room was comfortably sloppy. The walls were lined with shelves cluttered with various collectibles: glass curios, antique steel banks, some old cast-iron toys, several rows of antique jars. There was a big-screen TV in one corner, its viewing area a bored, opaque eye. In another corner a bar was set up. There were telephones sitting about like ashtrays; nobody would have to get up from any of the plushy upholstered black chairs in order to take a call. A well-fed yellow cat lounged on the arm of a black sofa, its head turned and drawn back tightly to stare at Nudger with calm disdain, as if on its list of things due respect, Nudger ranked far below litter box. New Orleans had no shortage of cats, and they all seemed to share the same low opinion of Nudger.

The dark-haired man saw Nudger and stood up. He was medium height, broad-shouldered yet very thin, younger-looking than Nudger had anticipated, with an even-featured face that was handsome despite deep acne scars that mottled his cheeks. He looked at Nudger with rather large, clear brown eyes. His expression was the same as the cat's. So was his complexion; his flesh had a yellowish tinge to it. He said, "Sit down, Mr. Nudger." His voice carried just the hint of a lisp.

As he spoke, a tall, chestnut-haired woman, who'd been sitting outside Nudger's range of vision, stood up.

"I'll be back in a few hours, darling," she said to the yellowish man and strutted from the room, regal and brassy as a showgirl. She appeared to have been crying, but it probably served to make her more beautiful, human as well as statuesque. Mrs. Collins?

As the door closed behind the woman, Frick placed a hand on Nudger's shoulder and guided him to one of the black chairs. The chair hissed as Nudger settled into it; he felt oddly helpless, a prisoner of all that softness, which would inhibit any quick movement. Frick backed away to stand to the side and slightly behind Nudger. Frack took up position by the door, crossing his arms in a casual but vigilant they-shall-not-pass attitude.

"I'm David Collins," the yellowish man said, walking over to stand in front of Nudger. He was wearing well-tailored dark-blue dress slacks, a silky blue-on-blue shirt, and crinkly leather gray shoes that looked suspiciously like house slippers. His clothes clashed with his complexion but his drink didn't. In his right hand was an on-the-rocks glass with a pebbled clear bottom; the glass contained ice cubes and about a quarter of an inch of diluted amber liquid, probably Scotch. He said, in a very calm and conversational tone, so softly, "Who has my daughter, Mr. Nudger?"

"I don't know."

"What *do* you know?"

"That she's gone. I was at Fat Jack's when you called him. He couldn't hide what the conversation was about."

"Willy Hollister's gone, too."

"Is he?" Nudger decided to play ignorant on that one, for Fat Jack's sake.

Collins grinned—no, grimaced toothily. When he did that he reminded Nudger of a young, sickly Richard Widmark. "His clothes are gone from his apartment. He didn't give his landlord any notice. He didn't leave a note or forwarding address. Just packed and left." He took a very delicate sip of his drink; nibbled at it, really. "Just what do you make of it, Mr. Nudger?"

"Are Ineida's clothes gone?"

Collins nodded slightly in vague admiration. "A sensible question. The answer to it is what disturbs me a great deal. Her clothes are there. All of her personal effects are there. Everything but Ineida. This is no joke that she's playing along with." A kind of slow anger seemed to be building in Collins, a modulated rage that sizzled with dangerous energy. Nudger understood why people feared him. "She's been kidnapped; I received a ransom note."

"Demanding how much?"

"Nothing specific yet. I'm supposed to be contacted again to let me know how much getting Ineida back will cost me, and where to deliver the money." He took another dainty sip of his drink; the level of the liquid didn't seem to have dropped at all when he lowered his glass. "Off this room there is a wine cellar, Mr. Nudger. I'm proud of it for the vintages it contains, but it also serves another purpose. It's windowless, and completely soundproof. A person could scream like a Civil Defense siren in there and not be heard even here, where we are." The large brown eyes didn't blink, didn't waver. "Why did Fat Jack hire you, Mr. Nudger? And don't deny he's your client."

"Why deny what you already know is true?" Nudger said, reasonably and in the interest of self-preservation. "He hired me to find out about Willy Hollister. He was worried about Hollister's relationship with Ineida, worried about what you might do if something happened to her because of her connection with the club. He knew he was supposed to be looking out for her, but there really was no way he could do that. The next best thing he could do was to find out where trouble might come from and try to head it off."

"And what did you find out about Hollister and my daughter?"

"Ineida is a nice kid who can't sing. And she's in love and not thinking straight."

"And Hollister?"

Nudger drew a deep breath and told Collins about Willy Hollister and Jacqui James and the other vanished women in various cities where Hollister had played blues as they had never been played before. The lines in Collins gaunt face deepened and his eyes darkened as he listened intently. This he did not like.

When Nudger was finished talking, Collins walked to a black steel file cabinet near the bar. He unlocked and slid open the top drawer all the way; it made a soft rolling sound on its tracks. Then he drew something out of it with his back to Nudger. He left the drawer open as he walked back over to stand in front of Nudger.

"Where did you get these?" he asked, holding out the stack of Ineida's love letters for Nudger to see.

Nudger thought about Collins' wine cellar, but not the wine. His eyes flicked to a heavy plank door that probably led to it. He still felt cooperative. "I took them from Willy Hollister's apartment," he said.

"You shouldn't be snooping around other people's apartments," Collins told him.

"Or hotel rooms."

Collins appeared puzzled for a moment, then smiled his Richard Widmark death's-head grin. "You got it wrong, Nudger, we didn't get these out of your room. Someone gave them to us."

"Who?"

"I don't know. They were mailed."

Nudger decided not to press. He didn't want Collins to press back harder, rock-against-Nudger-against-hard-place.

"How long have you had these?" Collins asked, hefting the stack of letters in his right hand as if he might decide to toss them away in disgust, out of sight, out of the equation of his life and his daughter's life. But he hadn't the power to do that, and it infuriated him.

"A few days."

"Did you show them to Fat Jack?"

"No." Nudger didn't mention that he'd told Fat Jack about Ineida and Hollister's impending elopement. He hoped Collins wouldn't ask about that. It would be client-protection time, and Nudger didn't know if he was up to it.

But Collins let the blame fall on the nearest target.

"Maybe Ineida wouldn't be gone if you had let me know about these letters. Or if you hadn't been hanging around asking questions, opening cans of worms." His upper lip curled nastily, slurring his words. He looked as if he'd encountered a foul odor.

"Listen," Nudger began to implore.

"You listen, you bastard! Somebody snatched my daughter. That means two things: First, I do everything and anything to get her back. Second, I do everything possible and then some to see that whoever took her lives long enough to regret it but not much longer."

"Call the police," Nudger said.

"Oh?" Collins began to pace back and forth. The yellow cat watched him without blinking, moving its head slowly left to right to left. "Is that an order, Nudger?"

"Advice. Despite what you read or see on TV, the best thing to do when someone is kidnapped is to get the police in on it. Then the FBI. They know their business."

"I don't want the law to know about this."

"Livingston knows."

Collins didn't answer. He didn't seem to think of Livingston as the law.

"I like your daughter," Nudger said. "I want to see her home safe, too."

"Good. That works out fine. It gives you double incentive."

"Incentive to do what?" But Nudger knew what Collins had in mind.

"You're a detective," Collins said. "You find out things. You're going to find out where Ineida is. You're going to get her back home, safe."

"That might not be something I can accomplish, no matter how hard I try."

"You'll wish it were. Because if, after a length of time I decide upon, Ineida isn't back here with you, you'll be back here by yourself. That will leave you with two stops to make: the wine cellar, and the bayou." He glanced somberly at Frick and Frack. "You'll look forward to the bayou, Nudger."

"You might be asking the impossible," Nudger said.

Black laser light glinted Collins' eyes. "Nothing's

impossible where my daughter's concerned." The ice in his glass made a tiny clinking sound; his hand was trembling.

He abruptly held the glass in front of him cupped in both hands, and turned away.

Frick stood aside and Frack made a motion with his big arm, signaling Nudger to leave with them.

Nudger was ready. The chair hissed at him like a malevolent serpent as he stood up. Frick and Frack waited while he moved through the doorway ahead of them. He glanced back before their oversized forms blocked his view.

Collins was standing on the other side of the room, still half turned away from them, holding and stroking the yellow cat. Both of them wore expressions suggesting they were dreaming of mice.

XXVII

Wise men purport to see a universality in all experience, a kind of connective tissue that exists throughout the universe so that no occurrence is independent of any other; there is, so they say, a reason for everything, and if one scrutinizes carefully enough, it is the same reason. These are wise men. Nudger was the kind of guy who was always trying mentally to recreate the day so he could figure out where he'd misplaced his car key, only to walk where he needed to go and then later find the key still in the ignition, where he'd forgotten it the night before. He often reflected that he wasn't cut out for his profession. But then how many people other than jockeys and bearded ladies were suited to their jobs?

And here he was, searching for the single connective reason in this universe of grits and graft that he'd stumbled into so willingly in order to pay next month's rent. To be able to find out what he didn't know, he needed to find out why he didn't know it. And the easiest way to do that was to get someone to tell him.

He had phoned Sandra Reckoner at several places, and

finally located her where he should have looked to begin with, at her home number. She was just like ignition keys.

She agreed to meet him for lunch at The Instrumental, in the same block as her husband's flagship antique shop, the lounge where they had talked about sex and ill-kept secrets.

Though the place was crowded, she'd been able to get the table they'd sat at before. The same husky waitress was gliding like a Roller Derby queen among the tables; the same musical instruments were suspended from the ceiling and mounted on the walls. The thing that was different was that there was a piano player now, and a young blond girl sitting on the piano with a drink and cigarette balanced in the same hand, singing Helen Morgan style. She wasn't bad, Nudger decided, but she needed her own act. That could be said of so many people.

Sandra looked cool and faintly amused. Her makeup and the dim light took ten years off her elongated face, robbing it of character rather than improving her looks. She had on slacks and a brilliantly striped, loose-fitting silky blouse with black half-dollar-size buttons; only a tall woman could wear that outfit.

"Did you decide you owe me lunch?" she asked Nudger, as he sat down across the table from her. The glass before her was empty except for half-melted ice. She'd been there awhile waiting for him.

"I owe you more than that," he told her. "Or maybe we're more even than I'd thought." The girl on the piano moaned softly about lost love.

Sandra didn't ask him what he meant by that; she was a great believer in letting time do its work. Nudger would get around to what he wanted to say, and she'd still be there to listen.

The waitress suddenly hovered over their table, pencil

poised. She was wearing perfume that smelled overpoweringly of lilacs. Avon screaming.

"Can I getcha anything?" she asked.

"Anything? Probably not," Nudger told her. "Just food or drink."

Her bored-waitress expression didn't change. Wrong wavelength, wrong planet. More evidence that the universe was made up of random, disparate parts.

"I'm not hungry," Sandra said. "I'll just have another Scotch and water." She looked at Nudger. "Go ahead and order some lunch; I won't think you're impolite."

"What's good here?" Nudger asked the waitress.

"Roast-beef sandwiches."

"What else do you serve?"

She shook her head. "Just roast-beef sandwiches."

"Good," Nudger said. A painless and easy choice was refreshing. "I'll have one with ketchup, salt and pepper, no onions."

"They only come one way," the waitress said.

No choice at all was necessary. "Great!" He wasn't being sarcastic; he was obviously really pleased about the sandwiches' lack of variety.

She looked at him oddly and made a darting squiggle of some sort in her order pad. She made similar marks to represent the drink orders, then moved away busily to deliver her message so that someone who read waitressese could interpret and cook and pour.

"The roast-beef sandwiches here are delicious," Sandra assured him. "Now that your mind's at ease about that, what else is worrying you?"

"Do I look worried?"

She nodded her long head. "And puzzled. About what?"

"Why were you waiting for me in my hotel room night before last?" he asked her.

She smiled. "I like you and I like lust."

"I don't doubt the last part," Nudger told her.

She seemed more amused than offended. "There's nothing wrong with lust; it's so much purer and less complicated than love. But why do you doubt the first part of what I said? I do like you."

"But you must know that David Collins doesn't share your affection for me. So why did you give him the letters?"

"David Collins? Letters?"

"Collins is the guy who sent you to search my room and my mind."

"And the letters?"

"The stack of blue envelopes you took from my room and gave him."

As he watched her face, Nudger's stomach began to bother him, a vague stirring of pain and regret. He was wrong about this woman, his stomach was telling him. A presage of guilt twisted its claws into him. It had to be her, and yet it wasn't. He knew it in that instant. He was hurting someone who cared for him, who had trusted him more than he'd trusted her. Yet he had no choice; he had to find out about this for sure, and then probe deeper.

"Is this the big-shot David Collins who gets his name in the papers now and then for charity and chicanery?"

Nudger nodded.

"Never met the man. These his letters that are missing from your room?"

"Not his letters, but they were written by someone he knows."

"And you think I went to you so I could pick your brain

and rummage through your room, that I used sex as an excuse to get in and stay awhile." She seemed, more than anything else, disappointed in him. "You believe I stole from you."

"I don't know that for sure. That's why I wanted to talk with you." Too late for moderation; he had lost her.

She stood up from her chair, looking down frowning and slowly shaking her head at him, as if he were vintage wine that had suddenly gone to vinegar. He had let her down in a way not so dissimilar.

"In the grand scheme of things," she told him calmly, "we didn't have much between us, Nudger, but what we did have, you've broken."

"I didn't have any choice. I had to know."

"And do you know?"

He did know; he was certain. It hadn't made sense from the beginning. "You didn't take the letters," he told her. "Sit back down, Sandra. Please."

She gave him a distant, pitying smile, turned, and walked with her long-legged stride through the crowd of drinkers and diners toward the exit. A one-chance woman walking from his life. Afternoon brilliance and traffic noise erupted around her briefly, as if she had magically summoned it all simply by touching the doorknob; then she disappeared into the brightness and sound even before the door swung closed.

Nudger felt suddenly as if the chain-smoking, chain-drinking, moaning girl on the piano were singing just for him. He sat morosely, thinking that the conversation hadn't turned out at all as he'd planned. In fact, a number of incidents had gone wrong for him lately. It was dispiriting; he felt dejected and small. Maybe he'd commit suicide by leaping from his chair onto the floor.

He tried to shake that feeling. It was counter-productive, and he had work to do.

Besides, maybe his string of bad luck was ended. Luck was like that—streaky. And it had balance, a way of equalizing. So probably, despite how he felt about what had happened with Sandra, he'd bottomed out and fortune was now on the upswing. It had to be that way; from now on, things large and small would break his way. He was, in fact, convinced of it. He could feel his new run of luck throbbing in his veins.

A shadow fell across the table. Sandra's? He jerked his head around to look up and behind him, caught the oppressive scent of lilac.

The big waitress was standing over him, looking blankly down at him.

She said, "We're out of roast beef."

XXVIII

Nudger didn't know the woman crossing the Majestueux lobby's deep carpet with a springy, indomitable sort of walk. Preoccupied with his problems, he didn't pay much attention to her until she got nearer. She was in her mid-forties, still attractive in the fragile way of blond women with porcelain complexions. Age had touched her lightly but often, a faint but harsh line here, a lack of luster in the well-coiffed hair there. She seemed brittle yet gentle and knowing, tempered by life's fire. Her springy walk was compact and graceful, like a gymnast's. She was on the short side, petite, and when she locked gazes with Nudger her pace toward him quickened. She had to be—

"I'm Marilyn Eeker, Mr. Nudger," she said. "The desk clerk pointed you out to me. I've been trying to get in touch with you."

"I know," Nudger said. "We seem to be a second behind or ahead of each other. Why have you been looking for me, Miss Eeker?"

"Mrs.," she corrected. "It's about Ineida. I know you've been . . . looking into her life."

Nudger waited, wondering.

Marilyn Eeker smiled nervously and glanced around. "Can we go somewhere and sit down, Mr. Nudger?"

"Sure." Nudger motioned toward the hotel restaurant. She went inside with him, and the Creole Queen who was the hostess led them to a corner booth by the window. They sat looking out at the wavering heat rising like sultry dreams from the damp street.

Marilyn Eeker said nothing until the waitress had brought the iced tea she'd ordered, the glass of milk for Nudger. She added two exactly level spoons of sugar to her tea, then a squeeze of lemon, dropping the rind into the glass. Nudger noticed that the cuff of her blouse was frayed. When she had finished carefully and thoroughly stirring the concoction, she said, "Ineida's missing, Mr. Nudger. What do you know about it?"

"What I don't know," Nudger said gently, "is who you are, and why you think she's missing."

Marilyn Eeker was surprised; her translucent blue eyes widened. They were beautiful eyes, only just beginning to fade. Then she smiled apologetically. "I'm sorry—I'm not thinking straight these days. I'm Ineida's mother."

Nudger's hand reaching for his glass paused. "David Collins' wife?"

"I used to be. We divorced fifteen years ago. David managed to pull strings, keep custody of Ineida. I live alone now, and use my maiden name. David and I never see each other. But my daughter and I remained close; we became good friends. She confides in me, Mr. Nudger. She told me she thought you were working for her father, then she became unsure of that. Who are you? Who are you working for?"

Nudger looked across the table into the deep and relentless agony that was tearing at the fiber of this gentle woman. Her daughter was missing, and she'd been left out of the game entirely. He figured he owed her answers. "I'm a private investigator, hired to look into Ineida's relationship with Willy Hollister. I can't tell you the identity of my client, but it isn't David Collins."

She gazed out the window for a moment, then turned again to face him and nodded. "I've met Willy Hollister. Ineida brought him by my house to show him off one day. I didn't like him."

"Why not?"

"I grew up on the bayou, Mr. Nudger, then went to school in the East and got sophisticated and came back still a Southern girl and snagged the eligible David Collins for a husband. My father was a naturalist. He used to keep alligators from the time they were barely hatched to when they grew big and wild and something made them return to the swamp. They'd get a look in their eyes just before they disappeared into the bayou behind our house; something would enter their minds that they couldn't control and didn't want to. I hadn't seen that look since I was a tomboy bending saplings, until I met Willy Hollister."

"How did you find out Ineida's missing?" Nudger asked.

"She was supposed to meet me and didn't show up. I phoned, got no answer, and went by her apartment. It was obvious she hadn't been there for a while. I called David, demanded to know where she went. He was evasive. He also acted as if something was very wrong; he couldn't hide it. There's a rage boiling just under his skin, Mr. Nudger. He gets that way when he's helpless, frustrated, and a little scared."

"Willy Hollister's gone, too," Nudger said. "It appears that he and Ineida ran away together."

Marilyn Eeker gazed down at her delicate hands folded on the table, breathed out hard through her nose. "I was afraid of something like that." She looked up slowly. Her pale blue eyes were clouded. "Ineida's pregnant," she said.

Nudger lifted his glass of milk a few inches off the table, set it back down, and shoved it away, sloshing some of it onto his fingers. Cold.

"Christ!" he said. "How do you know?"

"She told me. She's known for almost two months. She's approximately three months pregnant."

"Your husband didn't mention that when we talked."

"He's my *former* husband. And he doesn't know. Ineida was afraid to tell him."

"I'm afraid to tell him, too," Nudger said. "Is she going to have the baby?"

"Yes, she won't have an abortion."

"She should," Nudger said.

"Maybe."

He sat quietly for a moment. It all made better sense this way. Maybe Ineida and Hollister actually had eloped; maybe the pregnancy forced them into it. The ransom note might not be genuine, might be the work of a crank.

But he knew that was highly unlikely. For Hollister, Ineida's pregnancy would only be an unwanted complication, a catalyst for more tragedy. Still, Nudger decided to keep quiet for now about the note.

"Have you considered phoning the police, Mrs. Eeker?"

"No," she said, "David would kill me." She said it

calmly and reasonably. She wasn't exaggerating; it was an assessment.

"What are you going to do now?"

She shook her head, bit her lip. "I'm not sure."

"Go to Collins," Nudger told her. "Tell him you know about Ineida and Hollister running away together. Tell him you talked to me, and I confirmed what you suspected. Whether you tell him about the pregnancy is one for you to think over."

"He'll throw me out."

"He won't. He knows that if he does, you might go to the police. Threaten him with that if you have to. Ineida's your daughter; you have a right to know what's being done to get her back. Your husband will explain. Tell him if he doesn't, I will."

"He'll be furious with you."

"If he weren't already, I wouldn't be giving you this advice."

Nudger watched her wrestle with her dilemma. Then she apparently reached a decision; tension loosened its grip on her tight, squared shoulders.

She said, "Thank you, Mr. Nudger," and stood up. From her cheap vinyl purse she fished out a pair of crinkled dollar bills and laid them on the table. They were faded and finely worn, not unlike Marilyn Eeker herself.

Nudger picked up the bills and held them out for her. "I'll take care of the check," he said. "I'm on an expense account. Please. It's the American way."

"It's nice of you to offer," she said, smiling down at him. She had such a delicate, crystalline smile.

Then, ignoring the money extended toward her, she walked briskly away, prepared to face her former husband's contempt, and bring his anger with Nudger to a peak.

Nudger could understand why she and David Collins weren't compatible.

XXIX

Nudger decided not to tell Fat Jack about his unsettling conversations with David Collins and Marilyn Eeker. The big man had enough to worry about and would hardly be reassured by the fact that Ineida was pregnant, or that Nudger was being pressured hard by Collins to find her before any harm came to her. Fat Jack knew that as Nudger's search for Ineida went, so went his own chances for survival. And everyone knew the odds on any kidnap victim turning up alive. In such circumstances a massive client, as over-wrought as he was overweight, could be a liability.

"So what have you found out, old sleuth?" Fat Jack asked from where he stood by his office window. He was leaning far backward, as if to look down at a particular angle, his huge stomach straining at his gold belt buckle. Nudger wondered if he was contemplating squeezing through the window and letting two stories of height end his problems. But something told him Fat Jack wasn't the suicidal type; he'd thrived too long making music in an indifferent and demanding world to fall into the self-destruct category. His theme song was survival.

"I haven't found out anything new," Nudger said. "That's why I'm here. Did Hollister have a regular dressing room or locker where he kept a change of clothes or any personal items?"

Fat Jack turned to face Nudger. The light streaming through the window made his gingery hair appear sparse, his huge head more bloated with fat. He looked unhealthy these days. "Hey, I never thought of that! Yeah, he's got no private dressing room, but he does have a locker. Down in the hall near the green room."

Nudger assumed the green room was the all-purpose place of faded paint and yellowed posters. "Is it locked?"

"There are three lockers," Fat Jack said, "all with combination locks. The combination's two left, three right, one left."

"For which locker?"

"All of them. Nobody's supposed to keep anything valuable in them, and I can't give every new performer a fresh combination, so I keep it so I can remember the numbers."

"Which one's Hollister's?"

"The one closest to the green-room door."

The desk phone gave a shrill scream and Fat Jack jumped. Telephones were making him nervous lately. Nudger could understand why. They were nasty instruments that might convey the wrong message, that might at any moment spring up on their coiled wire and bite fatally.

"I'll let you know if I find anything interesting," Nudger said, drifting toward the door as Fat Jack moved reluctantly yet with ponderous grace toward the phone. Fat Jack was sweating again; his white collar was dark up near the top from perspiration. Nudger was depressed by being around such agony.

Fat Jack tucked the receiver into his neck folds and

somehow nodded good-bye as Nudger shut the door. Nudger heard him say, "Hey!" in a relieved voice. This caller wasn't likely to bring bad news.

Downstairs, business was already beginning to build. Marty Sievers was behind the bar, studying a sheet of paper and talking earnestly with Mattingly the bartender. He glanced at Nudger but gave no sign that he'd seen him. Judy Villanova was serving some of the exotic pineapple-with-parasol drinks to a group of women at a corner table who looked as if they might be part of a tour group. When she moved away to return to the bar, she saw Nudger and smiled.

Sam Judman smiled too, nodding as Nudger walked past. Judman was on the stage with the backup band, getting his drums set up for this evening, back at his job. Not much time had been wasted in bringing back old blood after Hollister had left. Obviously, Fat Jack and Sievers didn't figure Hollister would return here to play piano.

Nudger found the lockers easily enough, lined along the wall just outside the door to the grimy green room where he'd had his conversation with Hollister and been granted the great man's autograph. They looked like secondhand lockers from a high school gym; they were beige and defaced with indecipherable graffiti. Near the top of the middle unit it was proclaimed in a scratched message that someone named Gloria liked to do something, but Nudger couldn't make out what. It was more titillating that way.

Nudger worked the combination dial on the locker Fat Jack had said was Hollister's. It rotated stiffly, as if it needed oil, but at the end of the combination it clicked and Nudger could feel the tension of the dial relax in his hand. He twisted the handle and pulled the narrow steel door open.

Inside, a black Fat Jack's T-shirt hung on one of the

hooks. A wrinkled and soiled tan sport jacket was draped over another. On the locker's floor lay a pair of run-down jogging shoes.

Nudger searched the jacket's pockets, then turned each shoe upside down and shook it. He didn't find what he was looking for, only a small brown spider that fell from the left shoe and scurried for cover.

Outside in the club, the band started in on a warm-up number. Nudger didn't recognize it, but it had a strong beat and Judman was going wild on the drums while the crowd, carefree people who knew nothing about kidnapping and murder, clapped in time. It was good to hear.

Nudger stood still for a few minutes in the warm hall, listening. Then he closed the locker door, twirled the combination lock, and left the club without going back upstairs to Fat Jack's office.

"You want what I can't give you, Nudger," Livingston said.

He leaned back behind the desk, framed by the gloomy view out the dirty window of his office. A large bird, probably a pigeon, flapped near the glass as if confused; Nudger thought it was going to hit the window, but it veered at the last instant and swooped out of sight. Maybe the view through Livingston's window was as deceptive from outside as from within.

"Why can't you give me the key to Hollister's apartment?" Nudger asked.

Livingston peered around the ever-present vase of flowers; this time they were ugly things that looked like the kind of plants that ate flies and raw hamburger. They were in the right place. "That apartment's a crime scene," he explained.

"No crime has been reported," Nudger pointed out.

"Yet."

"True," Nudger said. "Maybe I'd better report a kidnapping and make it official that a crime has occurred."

Livingston didn't like that suggestion, didn't like Nudger for making it. There was pressure on Livingston from opposite ends and both men knew it. "Don't push that line, Nudger," Livingston said. The hard glint was back in his slanted, beady eyes. Tough little bastard, that glint said. Mean little bastard.

"As long as Collins hasn't requested police help," Nudger said, "you're under no obligation to regard the apartment as an evidence site. You really have no business possessing Hollister's door key."

"You're the one who said I had a key to Hollister's apartment."

"You didn't deny it."

Livingston smiled. "Think of the things you don't deny but aren't guilty of."

"This isn't a question of guilt," Nudger said. "You searched Hollister's apartment and found out his clothes are missing; I was told that by a reliable source. You're the type that touches all bases. I'm sure there was a spare key and you located it. Or if there wasn't, you have a copy of the landlord's passkey."

"I haven't admitted being in Hollister's apartment," Livingston said. Nudger interpreted that as a good sign; the captain might be starting to cover himself, which meant he might be considering allowing Nudger inside the apartment.

Nudger was sure that by now Livingston not only knew Ineida's disappearance was a kidnapping, he'd also be in possession of all available information. Collins obviously had notified him unofficially, given him the details. Maybe he'd even gotten a speech outside Collins' wine cellar, as Nudger had. After all, they were both in the same business, which sometimes entailed locating kidnap victims, and Livingston was familiar with the territory. Livingston had to play dumb, even though Nudger knew he was anything but that. A mutually protective charade was required here, and Livingston was good at charades. Practice, practice.

"We have the same interests here," Nudger told him.

"Sure we do. But I don't want you mucking up things."

"Speaking of muck," Nudger said, "consider the swamp."

Livingston grinned and shook his head knowingly. "I'm privy to certain facts that you don't know about, Nudger."

"Some things I do know. I know that people who know where too many bodies are buried sometimes join the group."

Livingston smoothed a lapel with one of his little paw-like hands and gave that some thought.

"Do you have any kids?" Nudger asked.

Livingston shook his head no.

"Then it's hard for you to understand the way a father feels about his only daughter, how he might react out of gut feeling rather than logic. Powerful instincts are at work there. Primal emotions. A bereaved father might do just about anything."

"Do you have any kids, Nudger?"

"No."

Livingston snorted, almost a sharp bark. He scooted his chair back a foot or so on its plastic carpet protector and bent down out of sight. Nudger heard a drawer slide open.

Within a few seconds Livingston resurfaced above desk-top level. He was holding a shiny brass key. He tossed it lightly so that it landed flat, with a dull sound like a dropped coin that hasn't flipped, on the desk corner where Nudger could reach it.

"I'll get this back to you," Nudger said, picking up the key and slipping it into a shirt pocket.

"I never gave anything to you," Livingston told him. "But if I would happen to give you something, I'd make sure I had a duplicate so you wouldn't have to return it. So with luck I wouldn't have to see you again, even if what I didn't give you got you into trouble you couldn't get out of." He didn't so much as begin to smile as he said that.

"Confusing but protective," Nudger said, "like good legalese. I admire the way you cover your tracks, even if it's at someone else's expense."

Livingston smiled his narrow and nasty smile. "That's the secret of life, Nudger, someone else's expense."

Nudger had to agree. He'd paid enough to know it was true.

XXX

After leaving Livingston's lair, Nudger drove directly to Hollister's apartment on Rue St. Francois. He parked the red subcompact a block beyond the tan brick-and-stucco building and walked back along the narrow sidewalk. He wasn't sure there was a need for such caution, but he knew it might not be wise to have his car seen parked in front of Hollister's apartment. There were unfriendly players in this game.

As he walked toward the sunlit tan building, he adopted a casual air and glanced around. No one seemed to be watching the place, but that was hardly reassuring. It only meant that someone who knew how to conduct a stakeout might be watching. The few people Nudger passed on the sidewalk seemed genuinely uninterested in him, but since he had come to New Orleans, little had been as it seemed. As he approached Hollister's door, he stuck his hand into his pocket and withdrew the key. He didn't want to stand on the stoop wrestling with the lock any longer than was necessary.

The key slipped into the lock smoothly, with a well-oiled, soft ratchety sound; Livingston knew where to have good duplicates made. Efficient little bastard.

Nudger turned the key and was about to rotate the doorknob and enter when something slammed hard into the door near his left knee. He bounded to the side, whirling, a teenager again, weightless and agile. Scared.

"Sorry," she said, scooping up the red rubber ball that had struck the door and lodged in the bushes near the stoop. "Didn't mean to spook you."

She was about twelve, a scrawny black girl with immense pigtails that appeared to draw back the skin on the forehead and make her wide, wise eyes seem even larger. When she got older, if she put on some weight, she would be pretty, maybe beautiful.

Nudger managed to smile at her, mentally brushing her aside, and reached again for the doorknob.

"He ain't home," the girl said. Blatantly curious, she was standing in the middle of the sidewalk, staring up at Nudger.

"How do you know he's not home?" Nudger asked.

"I knocked a little while ago. My ball bounced in his courtyard and I wanted to get permission to go get it. Nobody came to the door, so I went back and climbed the fence and got the ball anyways." She tossed the ball up behind and over her shoulder with her right hand, snatched it from the air at eye level with her left. Grinned. Nifty. "I'm Midge," she said. "I'm a neighbor. Who're you?"

"I'm Mr. Hollister's cousin. My name's Nudger. What does Midge stand for?"

"Just stands for Midge, is all. What's Nudger stand for?"

"Truth, justice, even the American way."

"Huh? Oh, that's a lot."

"Gets to be a burden sometimes. Thanks for the information, Midge. Bye."

"You goin' inside anyway?"

"Sure. Cousin Willy won't mind. I'm supposed to meet him here soon."

"I don't guess he's been back since last night," Midge said. She turned, bounced the ball off the sidewalk, and started across the street.

"Wait a minute!" Nudger said. Too sharply. He was concerned he'd frightened the girl. But she stepped back up onto the curb and then came over to him, looking up at him with those born-wise, unafraid eyes. No walkover, this kid. "Did you see Mr. Hollister here last night?" he asked.

"Yeah. Said I did."

"About what time?"

"I dunno. I was in bed. My dad came home and got in an argument with my mom over headaches or somethin'. Woke me up. When I wake up late at night I like to stay awake. I look out the window sometimes 'cause my bed's right by it. I seen Mr. Hollister go into his apartment."

"Was he alone?"

"Sure. It was late. He was probably goin' to bed."

"Then you didn't see him leave."

"Nope." *Whap!* went the ball on the sidewalk, as she bounced it and effortlessly caught it. She was young, full of fire and fizz, getting impatient with this conversation.

"Was your window open?"

Whap! "Sure. It was hot last night."

"Did you hear any noise coming from here, Midge?"

"Nope."

"Think hard. Voices? Anything?"

"I always think hard. There was some comin' an' goin', maybe. Commotion. Real late. Or it could be I dreamed it. Or

217

maybe it was Mom and Dad and they made up. They do that sometimes."

A rust-primed old Chevy driven by a black man in sunglasses turned down Rue St. Francois, slowed as it passed Nudger and the girl, then drove on.

Whap!

Nudger hoped that, whatever the source or genuineness of last night's noise, Mom and Dad had become friends again. He liked Midge and figured she deserved some regular sleep and family unity. The noise she thought she'd heard might have been Livingston's men, or Collins', searching Hollister's apartment. Or it might have been Hollister and Ineida. Or, as she'd suggested, it might have been a dream. Like this entire case; dreams within dreams. There were as many different worlds as there were people, it seemed, and maybe this world or that one corresponded to reality. Or maybe none of them did. Maybe there was no reality. All dreams. Or was that too terrifying to think about?

"Where do you live?" Nudger asked.

Whap! "Across the street there. My window's in front. I like it there; you can see everything that goes on, even real late when nobody thinks anybody's eyes are on 'em."

Nudger looked up at the second-story window she was pointing to. It was uncurtained; a crooked, yellowed shade was pulled halfway down. She'd have a good view from there, all right. "Have you seen anything unusual going on over here during the past week or so?"

"Nope." *Whap! Whap!* "I gotta go." She began backing away, worm of youth wriggling.

"Okay," Nudger said. He was even more anxious to get inside now. "Thanks, Midge."

"Sure, Nudger." *Whap!* The red ball bounced ten feet into the air, described an arc out over the street. She twirled gracefully and closed on it like a young female Willy Mays, made a perfect basket catch over her shoulder, and ran down the shadowed street and out of sight. It was a great catch, considering she'd been looking straight into the sun.

Nudger opened the door and went inside.

The apartment was still. Its air was stale, as if it had been closed up without movement all night and most of the day. There was a kind of residue of cooking-gas scent that was often detectable in places that had been sealed tight for a number of hours. Nudger could take in most of the apartment in a glance, right through to the courtyard beyond the sliding-glass-door draperies that were opened to outside, where the sun lay in slanted gold rays across the well-tended garden. A large bee of some sort was flitting around out there, sampling blossoms. In the kitchen the refrigerator clicked on, humming softly and contentedly.

Nudger began nosing around. There was no sign that anyone had searched the place before him, but there wouldn't be. The people interested in Hollister's and Ineida's whereabouts were professionals. Wall hangings, kitchen utensils, the small and unimportant trappings of living were still here, but the larger and more personal items were gone. Only a ragged wool sweater remained in the bedroom closet. The dresser drawers were empty but for lint, and the desk in the living room was cleaned out except for a few blunt pencils and a folded piece of blank notepaper. Nudger spread the paper flat and used a soft-leaded pencil to lay graphite markings gently over it and try to pick up an impression of what had been written on the last, missing sheet of paper.

That didn't prove effective; it only seemed to work in detective novels and movies. There sure were a lot of misconceptions about this job.

He put down the pencil and stood up from the desk. This visit hadn't helped him much, only left a steadfastly reliable witness to swear that he'd been here under false pretenses, if the law ever forced the issue in court.

He decided to leave, yet a part of him wanted to stay. It was an eerie feeling, as if his subconscious were telling him something and recoiling from it at the same time.

From where he stood, one corner of the bedroom wasn't visible. He walked toward the open bedroom door. The bed protruded there; he couldn't see beyond it to the wall.

Slowly, he entered the bedroom and walked toward a point near the brass footboard from which he'd be able to see the other side of the bed. He'd never believed the hair on the back of anyone's neck actually rose, but his felt as if it were doing so now. He moved a few steps to the left, craned his neck cautiously, painfully, for a clear angle of vision.

The carpet on the other side of the bed lay flat and bare.

Nudger let out a long, hissing breath and rubbed his hand over the back of his neck in relief. He'd seen every corner of the apartment now; it was empty of any of the things he dreaded finding.

But when he turned to go he stopped and stood still, as if he'd walked into a wall of icy air. In the dresser mirror he could see the reflection of the hall and the sliding glass door, and beyond the door the sunny courtyard. The rosebushes Hollister had planted were still there, growing in a row alternating red roses with white.

But something was different about them. Now, at the end of the row, there were two white rosebushes in succession, then a red. Someone had dug up, then replanted the rose-bushes, but had neglected to replant the two end bushes in the same order they had been in. Had reversed them.

Nudger went to the sliding glass door, unlocked it, and stepped outside. The lowering sun was warm as well as bright; some of the rosebuds on the bushes had bloomed and their petals seemed virginal and fragile in the gentle light.

In a crawl space beneath the sundeck, several garden tools were stored. Nudger rummaged around in the shadows, found Hollister's long-handled shovel, and carried it to the row of newly planted rosebushes.

He dug almost in a frenzy, feeling his arm and back muscles tighten and ache from the effort, afraid the sickening hollowness in his stomach would get out of control if he didn't work hard to keep his mind off it.

Nudger remembered a case Hammersmith had told him about back in St. Louis. A guy on the east side had murdered a woman he'd picked up in a bar, strangled her, and then buried her in the woods. He'd been seen with her in the bar, and it bothered him that when the body was found, he might be tied to the murder. It bothered him so much that after two weeks he'd gone back one night, dug up the decomposed body, and removed the head to make identification from dental records impossible. Hammersmith hadn't said what the killer had done with the head; Nudger hadn't asked and didn't want to know.

But it bothered Nudger that anyone could do that to a woman he'd buried two weeks before. And it puzzled him. What was it about people like that? What was missing in their minds or hearts? He knew he could never do what the man on the east side had done. Nudger would rather die in the electric chair than do that. Really.

He was damp all over with cold sweat. Emotion clawed at his features. He didn't want to uncover what he was sure lay beneath the loose earth.

He kept digging

XXXI

Hey, old sleuth, you gotta get over here," Fat Jack told Nudger on the phone.

Nudger had only been back in his hotel room for half an hour, had stopped his uncontrollable shaking only a few minutes ago. He was washing the dirt from his hands and arms after digging in Hollister's garden. His hands were still wet when he answered the phone; he wondered if anyone had ever been electrocuted this way. "Where's here?" he asked.

"My office at the club," Fat Jack said, as if Nudger were crazy for having to ask. "I just got a phone call from David Collins."

"What kind of call?"

"I better tell you in person."

"Okay, I'll be there in twenty minutes."

"Great. Hey, I got real problems, Nudger. Ultra-problems."

"You ain't seen nothin' yet," Nudger said.

"Huh?"

"Al Jolson used to say that before he laid the really big number on the crowd. Same way Ronald Reagan."

"I know. So what?"

"See you in half an hour," Nudger said, and hung up.

He stood for a moment, shirtless, staring down at the dark spots of water he'd dripped on the carpet. Then he went back in the bathroom, finished washing, and hurriedly toweled his hands dry. He felt like switching on the ceiling heat lamp in the tiny bathroom; despite the inability of the hotel's air conditioning to hold back the warmth of the day, he was getting chills. He put on a fresh shirt, shrugged into his wrinkled brown sport coat, and left for Fat Jack's.

"I hung up on Collins just a few minutes before I phoned you," Fat Jack said. He was standing behind his desk, twitching around as if he were too nervous to sit down. It was warm in the office, too, but Nudger's chilliness had accompanied him there.

He waited, saying nothing. That seemed to make Fat Jack even more jittery. He was visibly miserable, a veritable Niagara of nervous perspiration. Ultra-miserable.

"Collins told me he got a phone call," Fat Jack said, "instructing him to come up with half a million in cash by tomorrow night, or Ineida starts being delivered in the mail piece by piece."

Nudger wasn't surprised. He knew where the phone call to Collins had originated.

Fat Jack grimaced with fear. It wouldn't let up; it was gnawing like rats on his insides. Nudger watched, fascinated. It was something to see, a huge man like Fat Jack being eaten alive inside-out. "Collins told me that if any part of Ineida turned up in the mail, a part of me would be cut off. He told me what part; it ain't gonna be what's missing from Ineida."

"It appears he scared you," Nudger observed.

Fat Jack raised his writhing eyebrows and looked dumbfounded. "Scared me? Hey, he terrified the livin' shit out of me, Nudger. Collins is a man who don't bluff; he means to do real harm to the friendly fat man. I mean, hey, I take him at his word."

Nudger walked around the office for a few seconds, almost preoccupied, like a boxer finding the area of the ring where he felt most comfortable. Near the desk corner, about five feet from Fat Jack, he stopped and stood facing the big man. For the first time he noticed that Fat Jack had too much of his lemon-scented cologne on today; it did nothing to hide the fear, only made the unmistakable sharp odor of desperation more acrid.

"When I was looking into Hollister's past," Nudger said, "I happened to discover something that seemed ordinary enough then, but now has gotten kind of interesting." He paused and watched the perspiration pour down Fat Jack's wide forehead.

"So I'm interested," Fat Jack said irritably. He reached behind him and slapped at the window air conditioner, as if to coax more cold air from it. There was no change in its gurgling hum.

"There's something about being a fat man," Nudger said, "a man as large as you. After a while he takes his size for granted, doesn't even think about it, accepts it as a normal fact of life. But other people don't. A really fat man is more memorable than he realizes, especially if he's called Fat Jack."

Fat Jack drew his head back into fleshy folds and shot a tortured, wary look at Nudger. "Hey, what are you talking toward, old sleuth?"

"You had a series of failed clubs in the cities where Willy Hollister played his music, and you were there at the times when Hollister's women disappeared."

"That ain't unusual, Nudger. Jazz is a tight little world." Fat Jack sat down slowly in his squeaking, protesting, undersized chair, swiveled slightly to the left, and glanced briefly upward as if seeking some written message on the ceiling. He found none. He swiveled back to face Nudger, making himself sit still.

"I said people remember you," Nudger told him. "And they remember you knowing Willy Hollister. But you told me you saw him for the first time when he came here to play in your club. And when I went to see Ineida for the first time, she knew my name. She bought the idea that I was a magazine writer; it fell right into place and it took her a while to get uncooperative. Then she assumed I was working for her father—as you knew she would."

Fat Jack stood halfway up, then decided he hadn't the energy for the total effort and sat back down in his groaning chair. "You missed a beat, Nudger. Are you saying I'm in on this kidnapping with Hollister? Hey, if that's true, why would I have hired you?"

"You needed someone like me to substantiate Hollister's involvement with Ineida, to find out about Hollister's missing women. It would help you to set him up."

"Hey, set him up for what?"

"You knew Hollister better than you pretended. You knew that he murdered those four women to add some insane, tragic dimension to his music—the sound that made him great. You knew what he had planned for Ineida."

"He didn't even know who she really was!" Fat Jack sputtered. Not a bad actor; so sincere.

"But you knew from the time you hired her that she was David Collins' daughter. You schemed from the beginning to use Hollister as the goat in your kidnapping plan."

Fat Jack wrinkled his forehead, raised pained eyes to Nudger. He looked genuinely hurt by this absurd accusation, disappointed by Nudger's inability to puzzle things out. "Christ, old sleuth! Where are you getting these wild ideas about the old fat man? Hollister is a killer—you said so yourself. I wouldn't want to get involved in any kind of a scam with him."

"He didn't know about the real scam," Nudger explained. "When you'd used me to make it clear that Hollister was the natural suspect, you kidnapped Ineida yourself and demanded the ransom, figuring Hollister's past and his disappearance would divert the law's attention away from you."

Fat Jack's wide face was a study in agitation, but it was relatively calm compared to what must have been going on inside his head. During the last few days he'd realized he'd bitten off too much to chew. His body was squirming uncontrollably, and the agony in his eyes was difficult to look into. He didn't want to ask the question, but he had to and he knew it. He had to hear the answer.

"If all this is true," he moaned, "where is Willy Hollister?"

"I did a little digging in his garden," Nudger said. "He's under his roses, where he thought Ineida was going to wind up, but where you had space for him reserved all along."

Time stopped, then took a couple of extra slow ticks, the way it does when something irrevocable happens. Fat Jack's head dropped. His suit suddenly seemed two sizes too large, as if a year of Weight Watchers had caught up with him all at once. As his body trembled, tears joined the sheen of perspiration glistening on his quivering cheeks. "How could you have figured it out?" he asked.

"When I found out the letters were missing, I suspected Collins' alter egos Frick and Frack, but that didn't make sense in light of further developments. Then I suspected Sandra Reckoner, but she didn't take the letters. Nobody else I knew of could have been in my hotel room. Nobody even knew the letters were there. Nobody but you. You stole them and had them delivered to David Collins to further implicate Hollister by making it appear that he and Ineida left New Orleans together. Then there's the fact that Ineida's three months pregnant."

"Huh? Pregnant?"

"If Hollister had taken her, he'd know about the pregnancy and would have used it for leverage. But it was never mentioned in the kidnapper's ransom demands."

"Ineida's got one in the oven? You sure?"

"One in the oven," Nudger confirmed. He'd never liked that expression. "Her mother told me. Collins' former wife. Marilyn Eeker."

Fat Jack said nothing for a long time. Then he said, in a very low voice, "Okay, I guess all that leaves me in deep shit."

"The deepest."

He raised his head slowly. His question was a plea for mercy: "What now, old sleuth?"

Nudger stepped forward and leaned down over the desk so he could look Fat Jack in the eye. "Where is Ineida?" he asked.

"She's still alive" was Fat Jack's only answer. Crushed as he was, he was still too wily to reveal his hole card. It was as if his fat were a kind of rubber, lending inexhaustible resilience to body and mind. Nudger couldn't help it; he found himself admiring such stamina in the face of relent-less pressure.

"It's negotiation time," Nudger told him, "and we don't have very long to reach an agreement. I not only did a little digging in Hollister's garden, I did some refilling. It's a busy place, that garden. While we're sitting here talking, the police are digging in the dirt I replaced."

"You called the police?"

"I did. But right now, they expect to find Ineida. When they find Hollister, Livingston will begin to fit all the pieces together the way I did and get the same puzzle picture of you. It might take him a while, since he has less than I did to work with, but he'll do it."

Fat Jack nodded sadly, seeing the truth in that progno-sis. Livingston was, if nothing else, a smart cop. "So what's your proposition?" Fat Jack asked.

"We both have a stake in Ineida getting back to home base safely," Nudger said. "You release her, and I keep quiet until tomorrow morning. That'll give you the advantage of a head start on the law. The police don't know who phoned them about the body in Hollister's garden, so I can stall them for at least that long without arousing suspicion."

Fat Jack didn't deliberate for more than a few sec-onds. He saw the only way out of the maze and intended taking it.

He nodded again, then stood up, supporting his pon-derous weight with both hands on the desk. "What about money?" he whined. "Hey, I can't run far without money." He added with supreme logic, "That's what all this was about."

"I've got nothing to lend you," Nudger said. "Not even the fee I'm not going to get from you."

"All right," Fat Jack sighed. He was pure resignation now, whipped like a tub of butter. Despite himself, Nudger kept feeling some semblance of pity for him. Something so buoyant and enormous, both physically and in talent and accomplishment, was an awesome and pathetic spectacle crashed.

"I'm going to phone David Collins in one hour," Nudger told him. "If Ineida isn't there, I'll put down the receiver, pick it up again, and dial the number of the New Orleans Police Department."

"She'll be there," Fat Jack said. "Hey, I promise." He buttoned his suit coat, gathered momentum, and headed toward the door. He had some moves left; that was all he needed, some.

He was within a step of the office door when it opened.

Fat Jack reversed direction, as if he'd run to the end of his string and rebounded, taking two steps backward without turning.

Marty Sievers walked into the office. He nodded blandly to Fat Jack and Nudger, looking as if he had no idea that anything unusual was going on here. Nudger knew better. The cards were all up now; bluff time was over. Sievers must have been outside the door for a long time, eavesdropping.

"No one's leaving here for a while," Sievers said. He said it softly, but it was an unmistakable order to be unfailingly obeyed. A threat. It was effective, even though he wasn't carrying a weapon. He didn't need a weapon. He knew it. Fat Jack and Nudger knew it. That was enough.

"I guess I don't have anyplace to go right now," Nudger said.

Sievers smiled a handsome, glittering smile. Leading-man charm. Dazzling. Nudger had never seen him smile like that. It was unnerving.

"You might have someplace to go you never thought of," Sievers said, still in that same soft voice. "And in a hurry."

XXXII

Y ou turn back from our objective too easily," Sievers
said to Fat Jack. "It's still obtainable." His tone was
clipped, as if he were talking about a military operation.

Fat Jack wasn't swayed by Sievers' concise confidence.
"Christ, Marty, this thing is blown. I mean, hey, let's face it
and get out while we can. I mean—"

"Shut up," Sievers interrupted. "Stay shut up." Patton
meets blues man, Nudger thought. New commander. Battle-
field commission. "I was outside the door. I heard everything you and Nudger said. This operation isn't scratched;
we simply have to tighten the time frame."

"Tighten what . . . how?" Fat Jack said, sounding vague
and confused. Obviously not Green Beret material.

Sievers was looking directly at Fat Jack, but at an
unnatural angle that kept Nudger fixed firmly in his periph-
eral vision. Nudger had never seen anyone do that before. It
made the flesh on the back of his neck creep. "We get in
touch with Collins as soon as possible," Sievers said. "We
collect what money we can within the next hour, before

Collins learns about Hollister's body being found and figures there's murder in the game and maybe his daughter's dead. He'll be more likely to balk at paying then and call in the law."

"Why is the money so important now?" Nudger asked. "Alive is better than rich, when you're staring at a homicide charge and the death penalty."

Sievers swiveled his head slightly to look at Nudger, keeping Fat Jack in sight to the side in that peculiar way of his. It was easier with Fat Jack because of his bulk, but the odd intensity stayed in Sievers' eyes. It was sheer concentration and calculation; his juices were flowing as they probably hadn't since Vietnam.

"The money's important because of who we owe it to," he said. "Fat Jack and I borrowed a lot of money to cover unwise investments made with the club's profits. We not only dipped into David Collins' till, we took out loans from people who administer their own death penalty to debtors who can't pay. And without that ransom money, Fat Jack and I can't pay."

"I ain't worried about that now!" Fat Jack said. "We can run from those guys easier than from the law. You get a murder rap on you, and kidnapping Collins' daughter to boot, and you got no place to hide, Marty. No place. Hey, don't you understand?"

"I understand that we're going to finish what we started," Sievers said. "We're ramrodding this through."

"Collins won't even know you're involved," Fat Jack said. "But what about me? He'll come straight for me. And we hang around here and get nailed by the law while we're trying to collect a ransom and everybody in Louisiana will want to witness our executions just for the entertainment value. You're underestimating Collins' influence."

"I don't care what happens to you," Sievers said flatly. "The operation is what's important."

"Certain soldiers are expendable," Nudger said. "Every good military man knows that. And this one's back in Vietnam; he'll take his objective even if it kills all his men."

"Some of us have the guts to do what needs doing," Sievers said, glancing over with contempt at Fat Jack. "This tub of shit was expendable from the beginning. I knew it would be that way; I know men. I had to do everything because he was too frightened. He was always making excuses, hiding behind his obesity. There's no sand in him, no will to do what's dangerous or unpleasant."

"Then you're the one who killed Hollister?"

Sievers grinned. "Sure. We led him to believe he was going to murder Ineida, then share the ransom money with us. He liked the idea of profiting two ways. Music and money. Not that he had a choice."

"Hollister's throat was crushed," Nudger said. "Like Billy Weep's in St. Louis. Did you use a karate chop on them?"

"Exactly." Sievers seemed pleased with Nudger's correct guess, as if he'd encountered an unexpectedly apt pupil. "I followed you to Weep's apartment and neutralized him after you left," he said. "We didn't want him to mention that Fat Jack was a close friend of Jacqui James. Fat Jack witnessed Hollister's murder of the James woman years ago in St. Louis; that's how we controlled Hollister, got him to agree to murder his next lover for money as well as art. Fat Jack could have fed him to the law anytime it suited."

Fat Jack's eyes were bulging; he was terrified. "You're saying too much, Marty!"

"It doesn't matter," Sievers snapped, and Fat Jack seemed to shrink into his bulk and was quiet.

"Why didn't you let Hollister kill Ineida?" Nudger asked.

"Oh, we intended to give her back to Daddy. It was the only way to keep Collins from spending the rest of his life using his resources to hunt us down and kill us."

"Then she really is still alive."

Sievers nodded.

"Where is she?"

"That hardly matters to you," Sievers said.

Nudger didn't like the way he said it. Sievers looked hard at Fat Jack, warning him, fixing him in position standing up behind his desk, the way an infielder glances at a runner on third base and freezes him there before throwing the ball to first for the sure out.

Nudger was the sure out.

His stomach jumped around in violent warning; fear ran like molten copper along the edges of his tongue and the back of his throat. Sievers, with a solemn, businesslike expression that was scarier than a scowl, was slowly advancing toward him. Time for some of that danger and unpleasantness. A good commander wasn't afraid to get his hands dirty. Or bloody. Best to neutralize the Nudger problem as quickly as possible, get it out of the way and carry on.

"Now, wait a minute," Nudger said. "Let's talk about this. Figure something out . . ."

"We don't have a minute," Sievers told him. "You saw to that. As it turns out, you committed a tactical error." He slid obliquely to his right, just enough to place himself between Nudger and the door.

Nudger considered yelling for help. But he could barely hear the music from the club downstairs. The office was almost soundproof. No one would hear him. No one would come if he called.

Sievers angled his body slightly sideways, suddenly was airborne and twirling, his right foot slashing out in what karate aficionados call a crescent kick. Nudger leaped backward and felt a brush of air as Sievers' tassled brown loafer arced past his face.

But the backward movement to avoid the kick left Nudger near a corner, with almost no room to maneuver. Sievers stepped closer again, setting himself for more explosive mayhem. He felt about killing with his hands—or feet— the way Hollister had felt about making music.

Nudger knew there was a single, low-percentage chance of staying alive. Not taking that chance would be reprehensible. Would be giving up. Forever.

He gulped down his terror and charged.

Sievers was caught off guard by this sudden attack from a supposedly subdued opponent. That was why he just grazed the side of Nudger's head as he danced nimbly from the path of the charge and chopped hard with the heel of his hand. Not a clean hit. But no problem for the old trooper. He actually laughed at this unexpected sport.

Nudger's right ear was numb and buzzing. His desperate surprise attack had gained him nothing. His back was literally against the wall now. In a very few seconds he would join Billy Weep.

Sievers was moving closer, crowding him, daring him to charge again, wanting him to charge, yearning to taste fully the violence he'd only sampled; his fighter's blood was up. The bland man's compact body was coiled inside his conservative brown suit, building energy to trade for Nudger's death. His eyes hardened; he cupped his hands in peculiar half-fists and crouched low to spring. He became very still. He was ready.

Nudger didn't hear the shot.

He doubted if Sievers heard it.

Presto, change-o! There was a round bluish hole just left

of center on Sievers' forehead. It might have been a magi-
cian's illusion or the special-effects magic of movieland.
Only it wasn't; it was real life. Real death. His body didn't
move, but the energy seemed to flow out of it; the intensity
drained from his eyes. He was his old bland self. Amiable
average Marty. The guy you'd want your sister to bring
home to dinner.

Nudger looked over to see Fat Jack still standing moun-
tainous behind his desk. Almost lost in the big man's right
hand was a tiny, small-caliber pistol that looked too toylike
to cause real damage or have anything to do with the hole
in Sievers' head.

Things weren't as they seemed; the gun had done its job.
Something moved in the corner of Nudger's vision and there
was a solid thump. Sievers' body dropping to the floor.

"He didn't leave me no choice," Fat Jack said in an
oddly breathless voice. "He was gonna leave the friendly fat
man for Collins. He went nuts. Shit, he might have even
killed *me* after he was done with you."

Sievers wasn't quite dead. His body began to vibrate
and flop around, his heels banging on the soft carpet with a
speed and rhythm Sam Judman downstairs on the drums
would have envied.

The sight horrified Fat Jack. He began to suck in air
deeply, unable to stop staring at Sievers. "It was you or
him," he said, still in his breathy voice. "I had to put my
trust in one of you, old sleuth. You or him." He lowered the
thousand-pound gun to his side; his arm hung straight, as if
strained by the weight. "Hey, you're my only way out of
this, Nudger."

Nudger wasn't sure about that, but he wasn't going to
differ with Fat Jack. He looked down at Sievers. People
shouldn't do this kind of thing to each other. It was all so

damned unreal; hairless bipeds running around on a spinning globe of matter, whirling through an infinite universe, loving and hating and killing each other when they were all they had in the emptiness. What was going on here? Never had death by another's hand seemed so wrong to Nudger, even though his own life had been saved.

Sievers went into violent convulsions then, his arms flailing and his fingers trembling as if electrodes were attached to their tips. Nudger's stomach began to flop in time with the body on the floor.

"Hey, Jesus, make him stop, Nudger!"

"I can't," Nudger said simply, staring mesmerized with Fat Jack at Sievers and the small hole that didn't belong in his otherwise unmarred forehead.

"Ah, Nudger, you gotta make him quit shakin' like that!" Fat Jack's eyes were wide and he was pale and perspiring; the loose flesh draped over his collar jiggled with his effort to turn his head. But he couldn't look away. His bulk began to quiver almost like Sievers' convulsing near-corpse. He was weeping, sobbing in horror. Nudger felt the old pity for him. It wasn't surprising, since he shared Fat Jack's revulsion for what had been done here. Death was never an easy thing, but this was grotesque. The entire room seemed to vibrate with the force of Sievers' convulsions.

Fat Jack glided out from behind the desk, approached Sievers with his moist eyes clenched almost shut. With tremendous effort he raised his arm, pointed the gun, jerked the barrel back as he pulled the trigger.

The gun made very little noise; a flat, slapping sound.

Sievers was unaffected. Fat Jack had missed.

"Oh, Christ!" the fat man moaned. "Oh, Christ! Oh Christ! . . ."

He moved closer, fired again. Again. A small hole

appeared near the base of Sievers' neck. He didn't bleed; there was no power left in him to pump blood. A little strawberry-colored froth built up in a corner of his mouth, like pink soap suds. Nudger's stomach lurched and he swallowed. This wasn't at all the way death by shooting appeared a million times a night on a million television screens; this death was soul-wrenching to watch.

Fat Jack was sitting on the floor now, his huge legs stuck straight out in front of him. His pants legs were twisted up on him; his ankles, clad in black nylon dress socks, were surprisingly thin. Great tears, as befitting such a huge man, were tracking down his face, dropping to spot his white shirtfront. He was clutching the gun tightly between his legs with both hands, as if he'd been kicked in the groin and it still hurt. He couldn't stop sobbing.

Sievers finally got finished dying and lay still.

Nudger continued to feel a subtle vibration. His heartbeat. He drew a deep breath and held it for a while, forcing himself to be calm. Then he took a step toward Fat Jack and looked down at him. "Get up."

Fat Jack couldn't make it by himself. Nudger had to grip one flabby, perspiration-slick wrist and heave backward as the big man floundered, almost fell, then struggled to his feet.

More composed now, Fat Jack wiped at his cheeks with his sausage-sized fingers. He dragged a forearm diagonally across his damp face. He didn't have to look at Sievers now; he couldn't look at him. He kept his gaze up, away from the floor. Nudger waited for the deep resilience to come into play.

After almost a minute had passed, Fat Jack straightened his mussed pants and shirt, ran his fingers through his thinning gingery hair, and looked at Nudger with the old light of pure reason back in his piggy little eyes.

"Same deal as before?" he asked.

Nudger didn't have any alternative. His primary consideration was getting Ineida back home alive and unharmed. Staying alive and unharmed himself. He nodded.

Fat Jack tossed the tiny spent revolver into a corner, moved to the desk, and began hurriedly stuffing his pockets with whatever he thought he might need and could carry. He knew the police were digging right now in Hollister's garden. Digging. Digging.

"I'm going to phone Collins' home in one hour," Nudger reminded him. "If Ineida's not there, my next call will be to the police."

"She'll be there. Hey, trust me. I trust you, Nudger."

"Neither of us has a choice," Nudger said.

"That's the way the world works, old sleuth. No choices. Not really. Not for anyone. Slide Marty's wallet out of his coat and hand it to me, will you?"

"No. You get it."

"I can't, Nudger. You know that. I gotta have *some* money! A man can't run far without the green stuff!"

"I told you before, I've got nothing to lend you."

Fat Jack tried again to look down at Sievers, but he couldn't make it. His head rotated slightly toward the body, but his eyes wouldn't follow; only the glistening whites were aimed at Sievers.

"All right, old sleuth," Fat Jack said resignedly. "I'm going on the cheap."

He tucked in his sweat-plastered shirt beneath his huge stomach, wrestled into his tent-sized suit coat, and without a backward glance at Nudger glided majestically from the room. Even the hell of what had happened here would soon be pushed to a far, dark corner of his mind; he'd have his old jaunty stride back in no time.

Nudger walked to the closed office door and locked it. Then he went to Fat Jack's desk and sat down. The soft sound of the blues filtering up from downstairs only made the office seem more quiet. He could barely see the toe of one of Sievers' kicked-off loafers lying next to a still, brown-stockinged foot. Death and silence had everything in common. Nudger would spend the next hour with these two, getting to know them better than he wanted.

He heard his rapid breathing gain a softer, steadier rhythm, and the pace of his heartbeat leveled off. The blues number he'd become involved in was played out now. Almost. Nudger settled back in Fat Jack's chair.

He sat with the man with the hole in his head and felt time crawl slowly over both of them.

XXXIII

When Nudger answered the knock on his hotel-room door the next morning, he wasn't really surprised to find Frick and Frack looming in the hall. They pushed into the room without being invited. There was a sneer on Frick's pockmarked face. Frack gave his boxer's nifty little shuffle and stood between Nudger and the door, smiling politely.

"We interrupt your sleep, my friend?" Frick asked in his buttery accent. He looked amused.

Their knocking had awakened Nudger. He'd made it out of bed, then slipped into his pants but not his shirt. He was bare-chested, bare-footed, digging his toes nervously into the rough carpet. He felt vulnerable, standing there without his shoes and socks on. His stomach, which a moment ago had yearned for breakfast, wasn't so sure about food now.

"Mr. Collins is of the opinion you saved his daughter's life," Frick said. "This came out very well for you, my friend."

"And for Ineida, considering."

"But Mr. Collins still isn't exactly fond of you," Frack said. "He don't like you personally, I guess."

Nudger ran his tongue around the inside of his mouth; he'd slept too long and his teeth felt fuzzy. He didn't like not being liked by David Collins. He wanted coffee. He wanted to brush his teeth.

"Mr. Collins thinks you're a guy who's habitually putting your nose where it doesn't belong," Frick said. "He's right, eh?"

"I don't put my nose anywhere," Nudger said. "I only follow it. He's afraid of where it might lead me."

Frick slowly shook his head. "Not afraid, my friend. Cautious." His eerie little smile took form as he said, "We brought you something from Mr. Collins." He reached into an inside pocket of his pale green sport jacket. At the moment, the coat just about matched Nudger's complexion.

All Frick brought out of the pocket, though, was an envelope. He held it out for Nudger, who accepted it and was surprised to see that his hands were steady as he opened it.

The envelope contained a single ticket for a coach seat on the 4:45 Amtrak *City of New Orleans* to St. Louis.

Frick said, "Mr. Collins wants you to take a train instead of a plane so you get the feeling of distance."

"I'll like that feeling," Nudger said.

Frick's smile broadened, lost its faraway, unsettling quality, and became genuinely friendly, even admiring. "You did okay, my friend. You did what was right for Ineida. Mr. Collins appreciates that."

"What about Fat Jack?" Nudger asked.

Frick's warm smile changed subtly, went cold. It became the dreamy, unpleasant sort of smile Nudger had seen before.

"Where Fat Jack is now," Frack said, "most of his friends are alligators."

"After Fat Jack talked to you," said Frick, "he went to Mr. Collins. He couldn't make himself walk out on all that possible money; some guys just have to play all their cards. He told Mr. Collins that for a certain amount of cash he would reveal Ineida's whereabouts, but it all had to be done in a hurry."

Nudger felt a coolness move over him, swirl around his bare feet. Marty Sievers had been persuasive enough last night to convince Fat Jack to try what he, Sievers, had been planning. But Fat Jack wasn't Sievers. Nobody was, anymore.

"He revealed her whereabouts in a hurry, all right," Frick said, "but for free." Astoundingly, he gave a sudden, soft giggle. A woman's laugh. "That fat man talked and talked. Faster and faster. In fact, he kept talking till nobody was listening, till he couldn't talk anymore."

Nudger swallowed dryly. He forgot about breakfast. Fat Jack had been a bad businessman to the end, dealing in desperation instead of distance. Maybe he hadn't had enough of the blues during the past several years, and too much of the good life; maybe he couldn't picture going on without that life. That was no problem to him now.

"You better pack, my friend," Frick said, gently patting Nudger's shoulder. "Train north pulls out on time."

Both men turned and left the room.

Nudger closed the door behind them. He looked at his Amtrak ticket in its red-and-blue folder. He looked at his bare feet. He looked at his wristwatch. There was plenty of time to catch the train. In fact, he had much of the day to kill. But he didn't feel like killing it here, or anywhere else where anyone connected with Collins or Sievers or Fat Jack or murder might find him. He decided to check out of the hotel, put his suitcase in a locker at the train station, and find some quiet place to eat breakfast where no one would bother him. Then he would walk around New Orleans for a while, listen to a little jazz played by the street musicians in the French Quarter, and maybe have a late lunch at the station before boarding the train for St. Louis and home and Claudia.

He showered, dressed quickly, and began to pack.

Two days after Nudger got home, he found a flat, padded package with a New Orleans postmark in his mail. He placed it on his desk and cautiously opened it.

The package contained two items: a check from David Collins made out to Nudger for more than twice the amount of Fat Jack's uncollectible fee; and an old blues record in its original wrapper, a fifties rendition of "You Got the Reach but Not the Grasp."

It featured Fat Jack McGee on clarinet.

THE RIGHT TO SING THE BLUES:

A Word After

by John Lutz

From the beginning I thought my home town of St. Louis was the perfect city for a detective like Nudger. It's a major city with a small town inferiority complex—not so much now, but certainly at the time this novel was written. St. Louisans, when traveling, felt a pang of hesitation before answering the question "Where are you from?" We feared the commiseration of those from Chi-town or L.A. or San Fran, or vacation spots like Miami or Las Vegas, or Eden-like places such as San Diego, where there is no bad weather; but most of all from NEW YORK CITY.

Not that St. Louis wasn't and isn't a great city to live in. In fact, it now enjoys a pretty good tourist trade with folks who've discovered its treasures and think it's a fine place to vacation. But it's long had the reputation of being a place not to be. Tennessee Williams liked it not at all and got out. As did T.S. Eliot. Three of Hemingway's wives were *from* St. Louis. If they could visit it now, I suspect they would feel differently.

But I thought it might be a good idea for Nudger to get out of St. Louis for a while, to do a little traveling. And where better for a hapless struggler of a P.I. than New Orleans, the city of the blues? Nudger is, after all, a guy who lives the blues. We all now and then have one of those days, but Nudger is having one of those lives. Besides, I had always liked New Orleans myself, so I figured it would be a cinch that Nudger would.

So, *The Right to Sing the Blues* explores the connections between people in both those cities on the Mississippi, people with problems and secrets. Most of both relate to a piano player whose music is on the side of the angels but whose life away from the keyboard runs more toward deviltry; and a beautiful young singer who doesn't notice the distinction.

I hope in this novel I've captured some of the tradition and flavor, and some of the commonalties, in these two intriguing cities. The past is very much alive in both, and haunts the mood and the people.

People who live the blues.

Nudger's people.

Nudger.